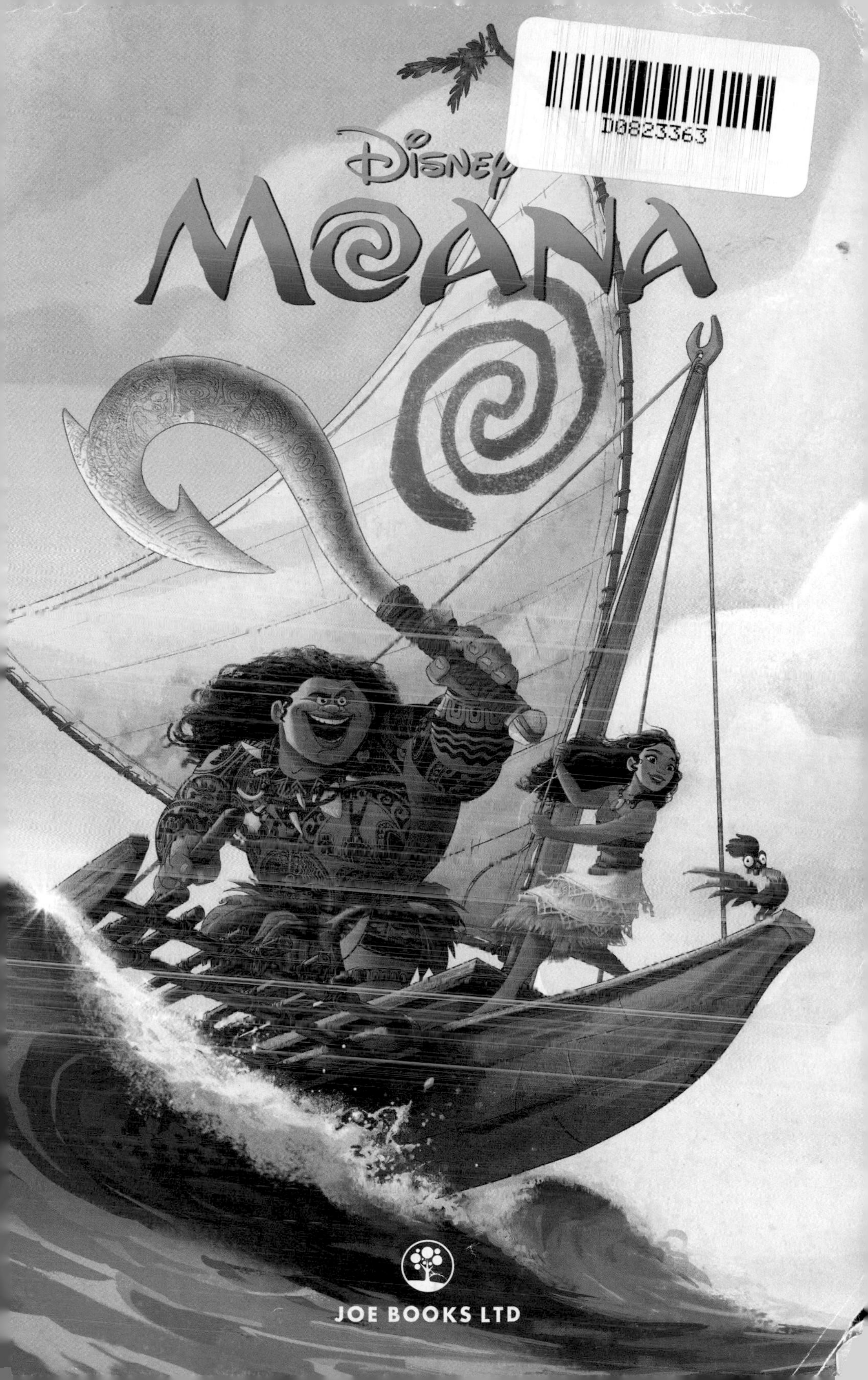
Disney
MOANA
JOE BOOKS LTD

Published simultaneously in the United States and Canada by
Joe Books Ltd, 489 College Street, Suite 203, Toronto, Ontario, M6G 1A5.

www.joebooks.com

First Joe Books Edition: December 2016

Print ISBN: 978-1-77275-295-3
ebook ISBN: 978-1-77275-479-7

Library and Archives Canada Cataloguing in Publication
information is available upon request.

Printed and bound in Canada
1 3 5 7 9 10 8 6 4 2

Disney

MOANA

TO ITS INHABITANTS, MOTUNUI IS MORE THAN JUST AN ISLAND—IT'S THEIR WHOLE WORLD, A PARADISE THAT GIVES THEM EVERYTHING THEY NEED. MEET THE ONES WHO CALL MOTUNUI HOME...

Moana

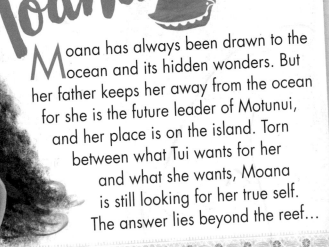

Moana has always been drawn to the ocean and its hidden wonders. But her father keeps her away from the ocean for she is the future leader of Motunui, and her place is on the island. Torn between what Tui wants for her and what she wants, Moana is still looking for her true self. The answer lies beyond the reef...

Tala

Tala is Moana's wise and unconventional grandmother who shares her special connection to the ocean. Tala knows well the heritage of her people, while most of the islanders have chosen to forget it. Her stories feed Moana's imagination and will help her make the right decision when the time comes.

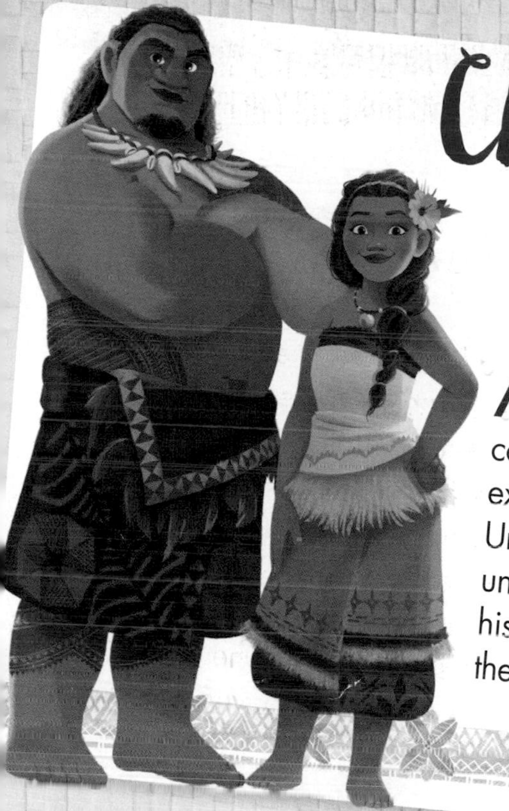

Chief Tui and Sina

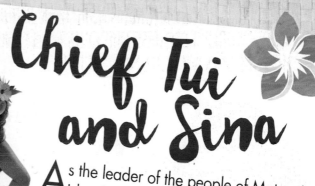

As the leader of the people of Motunui Island, Tui is only interested in the common good, which does not include exploring the sea beyond the reef. Unlike his wife Sina, Tui does not understand why Moana cannot just follow his teachings and learn how to become the next great chief of their people.

Heihei

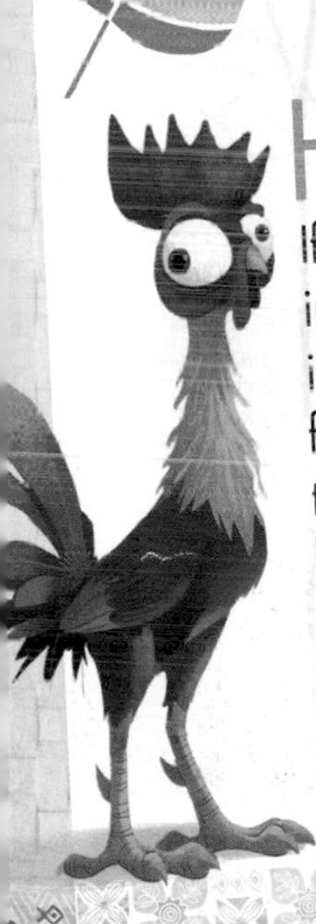

Heihei is not like any other chicken. He's dumber. If there's one way to get into danger, Heihei will find it. If there are two, he will find both of them. And still, there's no logical reason behind his actions. Yet, Moana believes there's more to him than meets the eye and that he does not deserve to be cooked and eaten!

Pua

This small, adorable pig is Moana's loyal pet & friend. Not afraid of water or boats, Pua is always ready to jump on a canoe to help Moana achieve her heart's desire: to reach the open ocean!

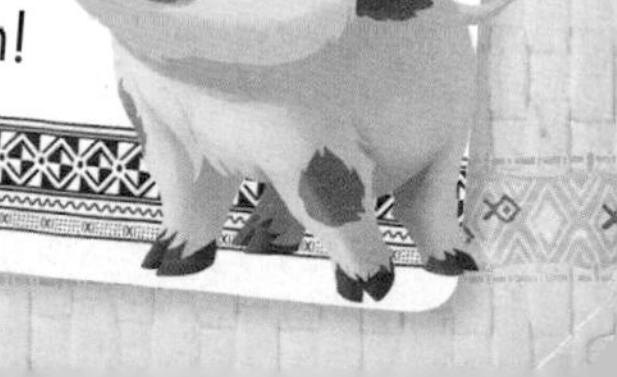

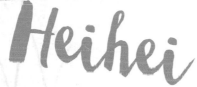

THE WORLD BEYOND THE REEF IS DANGEROUS AND UNFORGIVING, HOME TO HORRIBLE MONSTERS AND THOSE FAR MORE POWERFUL THAN HUMANS...

Maui

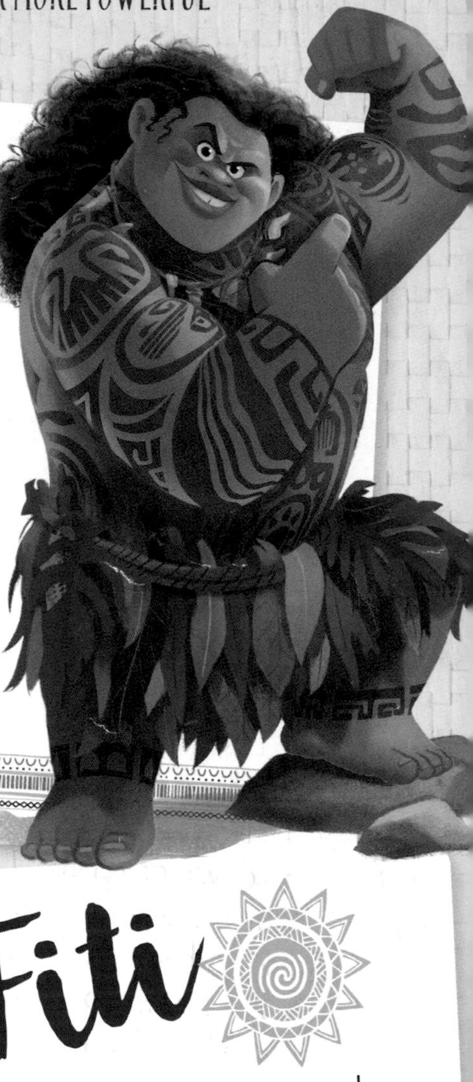

Once the greatest hero in Oceania, Maui is now just a legend, a forgotten demigod. After stealing the heart of Te Fiti, Maui has been confined to a small island, his only friend being one of his tattoos, a mini version of himself. Maui just wants to forget about his past and recover his magical fishhook, which allows him to shape-shift into all kinds of animals.

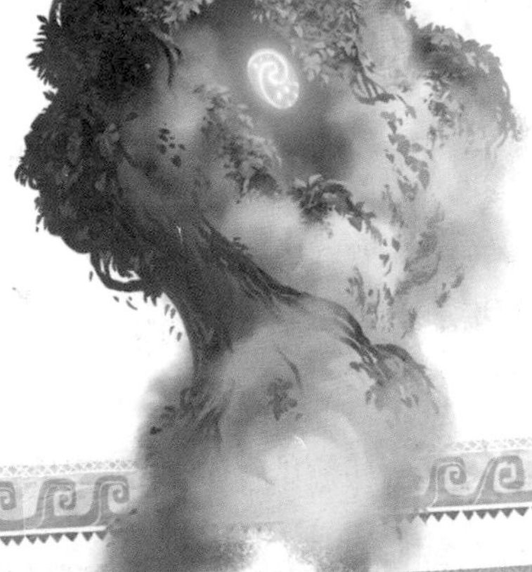

Te Fiti

Te Fiti, the mother island, emerged from the ocean at the beginning of time and created life. She made plants, humans and animals flourish. But when Maui stole her heart, darkness began to spread among the islands...

Kakamora

They may look cute, when you look at them from a distance, but these little warriors are just murdering pirates! They paint angry faces on their coconut-shell armor and attack any vessel crossing their waters to the dreadful beat of their big drums.

Tamatoa

Tamatoa is a scavenger, a collector of treasures, who lives in Lalotai, the land of monsters. He is obsessed with any shiny object that can make him as sparkly as a diamond. When Maui lost his precious hook, Tamatoa found it and added it to his collection.

Te Kā

Te Kā is a gigantic lava monster, a demon of earth and fire. Surrounded by ash clouds and volcanic lightning, Te Kā walks on land and cannot touch water. A very long time ago, Te Kā defeated Maui, separating him from his hook.

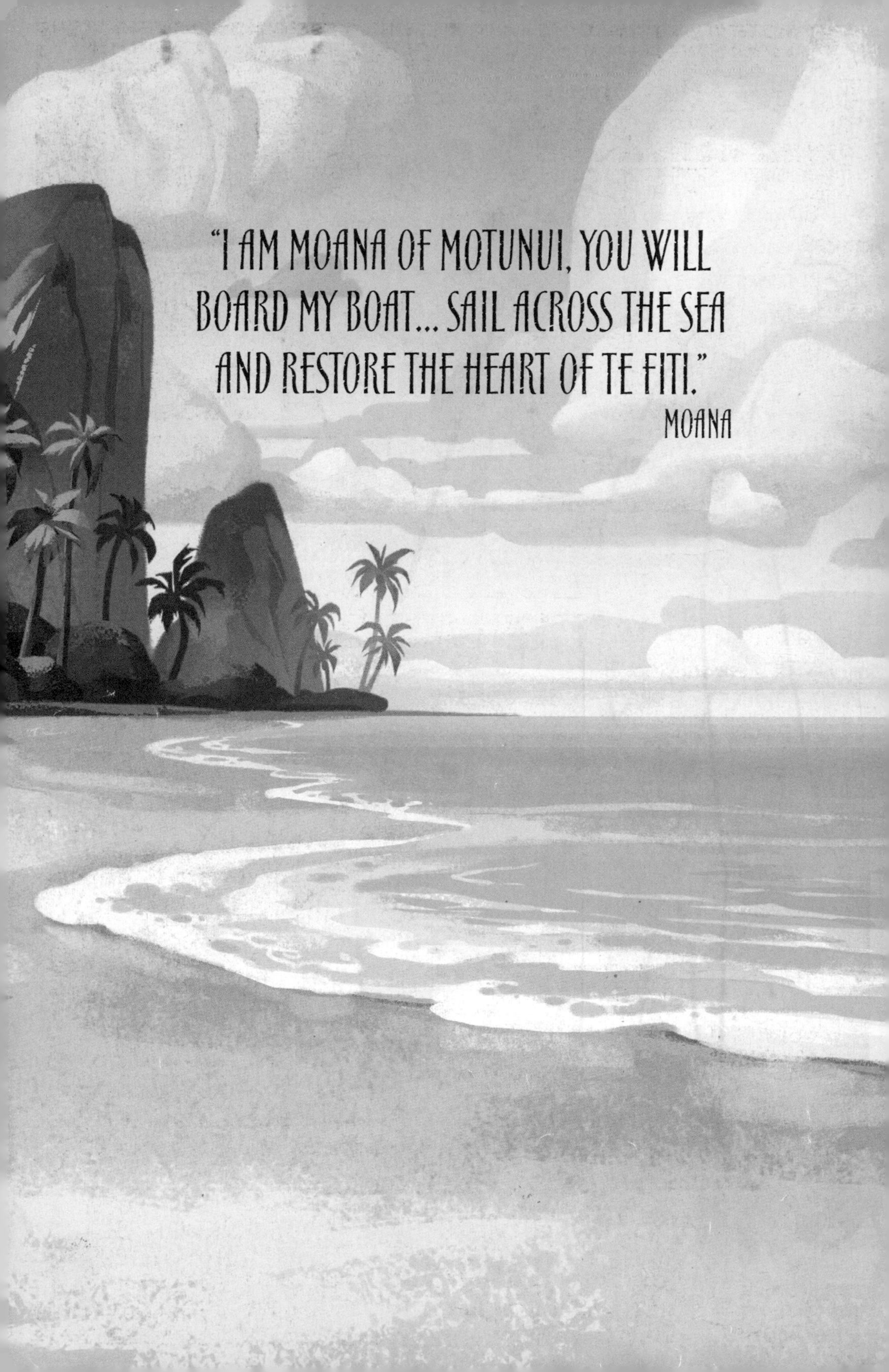

"I AM MOANA OF MOTUNUI, YOU WILL BOARD MY BOAT... SAIL ACROSS THE SEA AND RESTORE THE HEART OF TE FITI."

MOANA

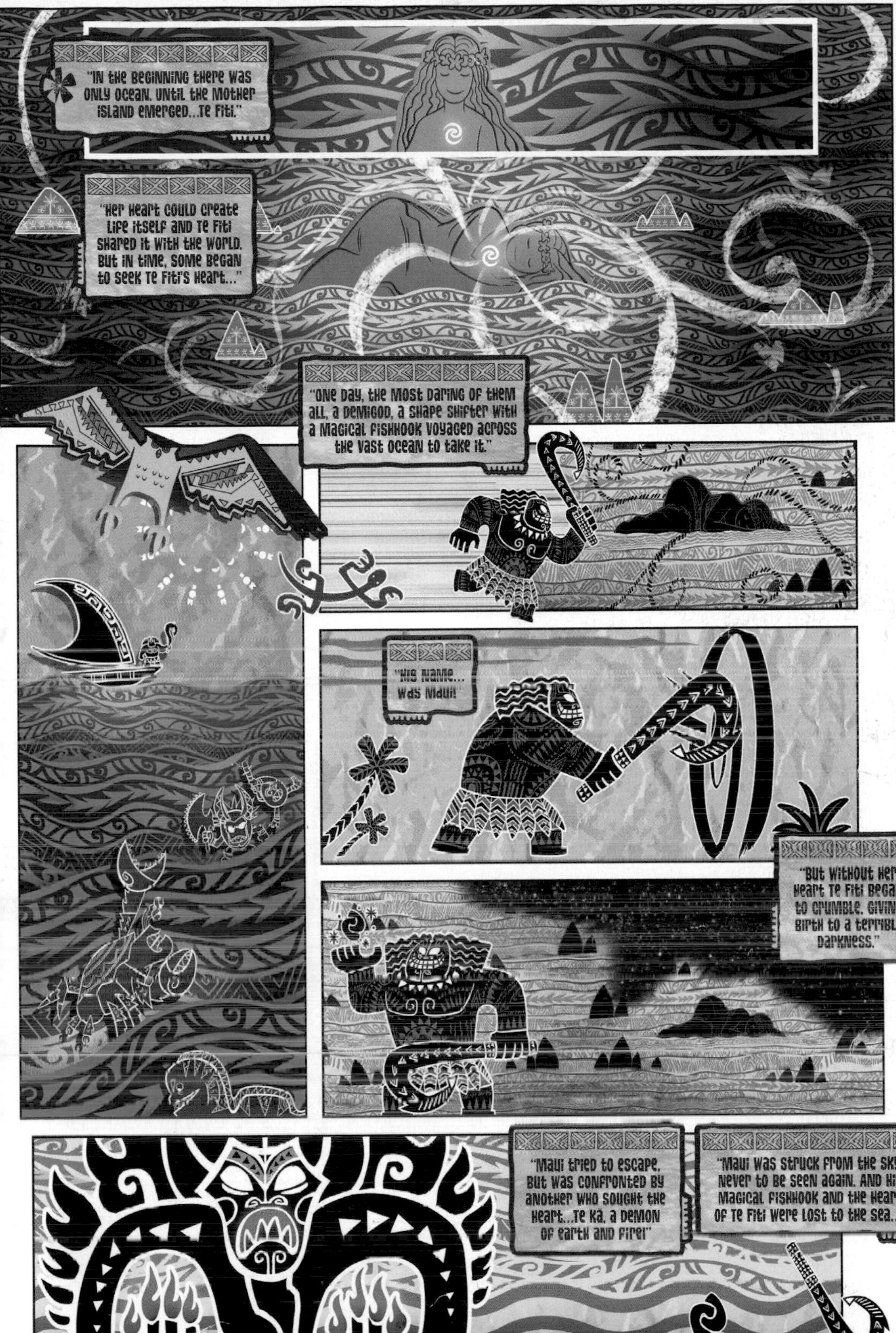
"In the beginning there was only ocean. Until the Mother Island emerged...Te Fiti."
"Her heart could create life itself and Te Fiti shared it with the world. But in time, some began to seek Te Fiti's heart..."
"One day, the most daring of them all, a demigod, a shape shifter with a magical fishhook voyaged across the vast ocean to take it."
"His name... was Maui!"
"But without her heart Te Fiti began to crumble, giving birth to a terrible darkness."
"Maui tried to escape, but was confronted by another who sought the heart...Te Kā, a demon of earth and fire!"
"Maui was struck from the sky, never to be seen again. And his magical fishhook and the heart of Te Fiti were lost to the sea..."

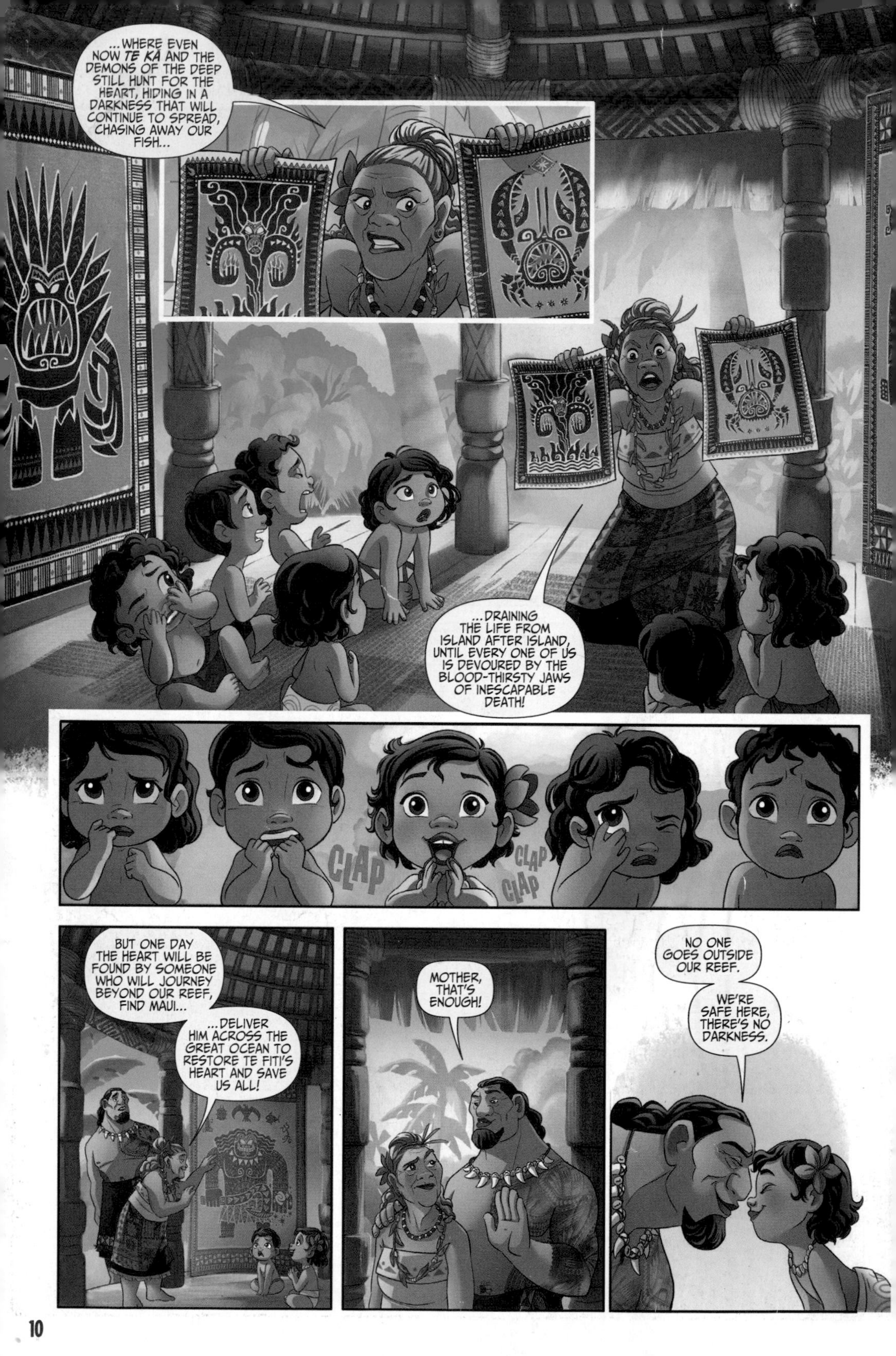
...WHERE EVEN NOW *TE KĀ* AND THE DEMONS OF THE DEEP STILL HUNT FOR THE HEART, HIDING IN A DARKNESS THAT WILL CONTINUE TO SPREAD, CHASING AWAY OUR FISH...
...DRAINING THE LIFE FROM ISLAND AFTER ISLAND, UNTIL EVERY ONE OF US IS DEVOURED BY THE BLOOD-THIRSTY JAWS OF INESCAPABLE DEATH!
CLAP
CLAP
CLAP
BUT ONE DAY THE HEART WILL BE FOUND BY SOMEONE WHO WILL JOURNEY BEYOND OUR REEF, FIND MAUI...
...DELIVER HIM ACROSS THE GREAT OCEAN TO RESTORE TE FITI'S HEART AND SAVE US ALL!
MOTHER, THAT'S ENOUGH!
NO ONE GOES OUTSIDE OUR REEF.
WE'RE SAFE HERE, THERE'S NO DARKNESS.

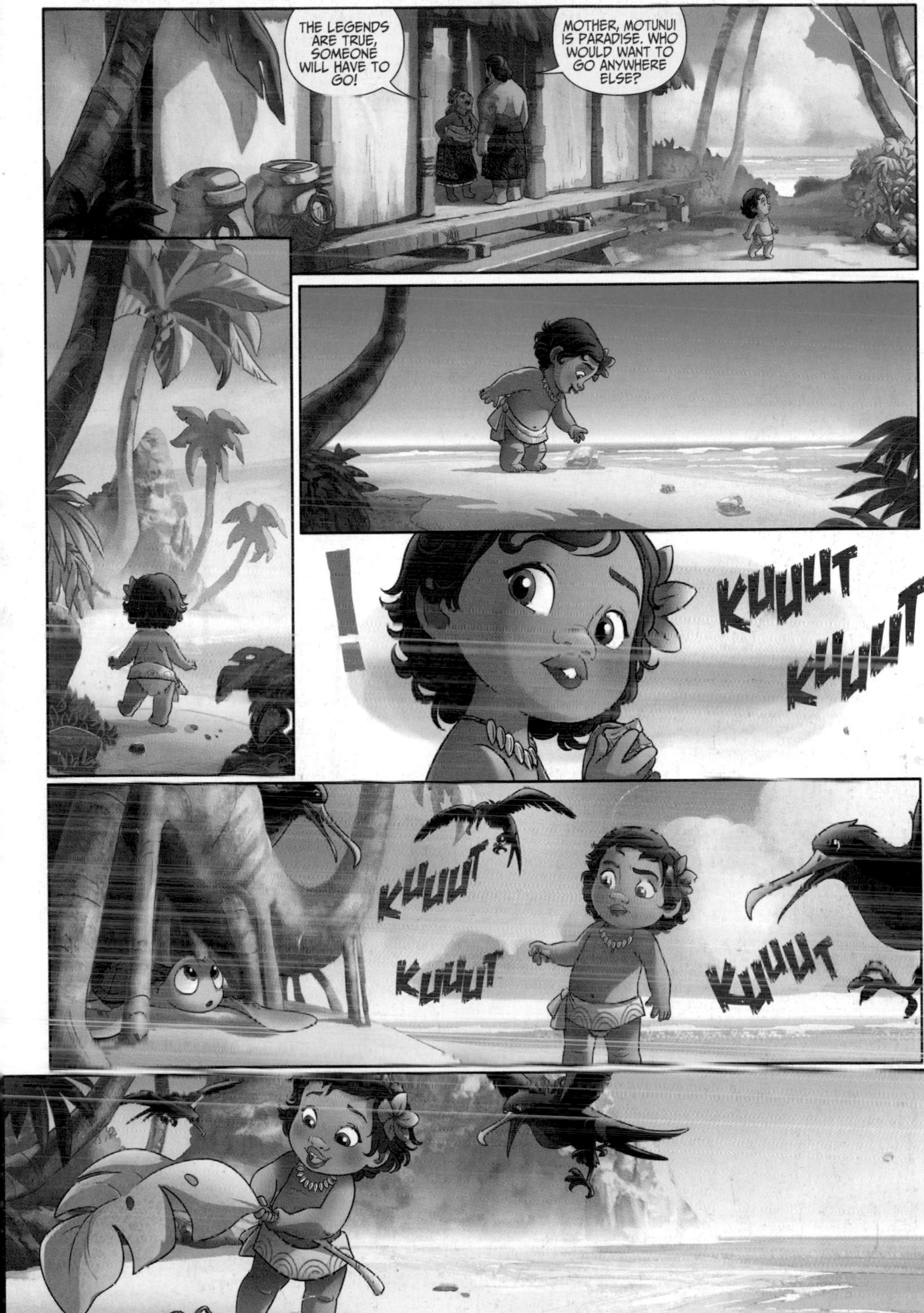
THE LEGENDS ARE TRUE, SOMEONE WILL HAVE TO GO!
MOTHER, MOTUNUI IS PARADISE. WHO WOULD WANT TO GO ANYWHERE ELSE?
!
KUUUT
KUUUT
KUUUT
KUUUT
KUUUT

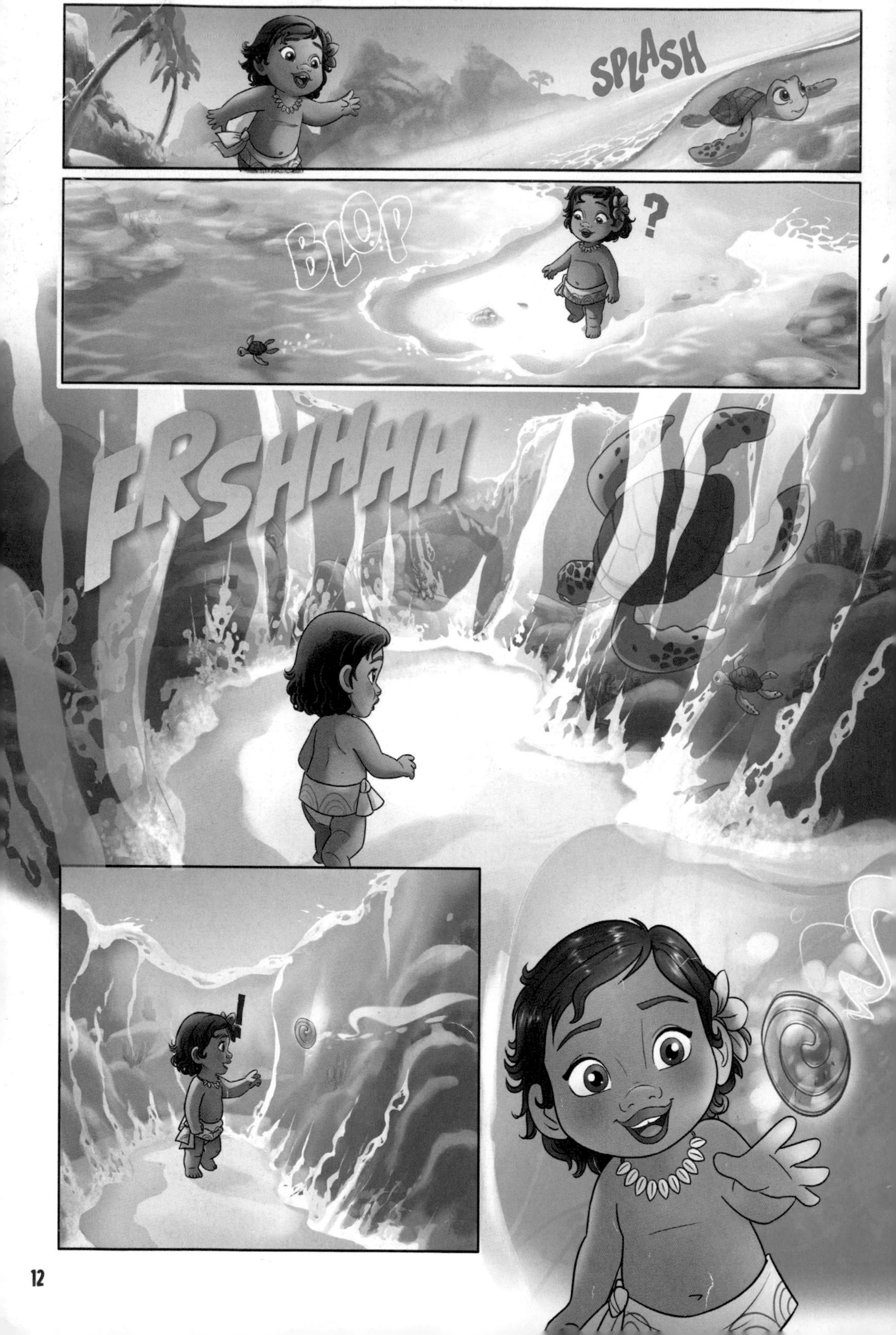
SPLASH
BLOP
?
FRSHHHH
!

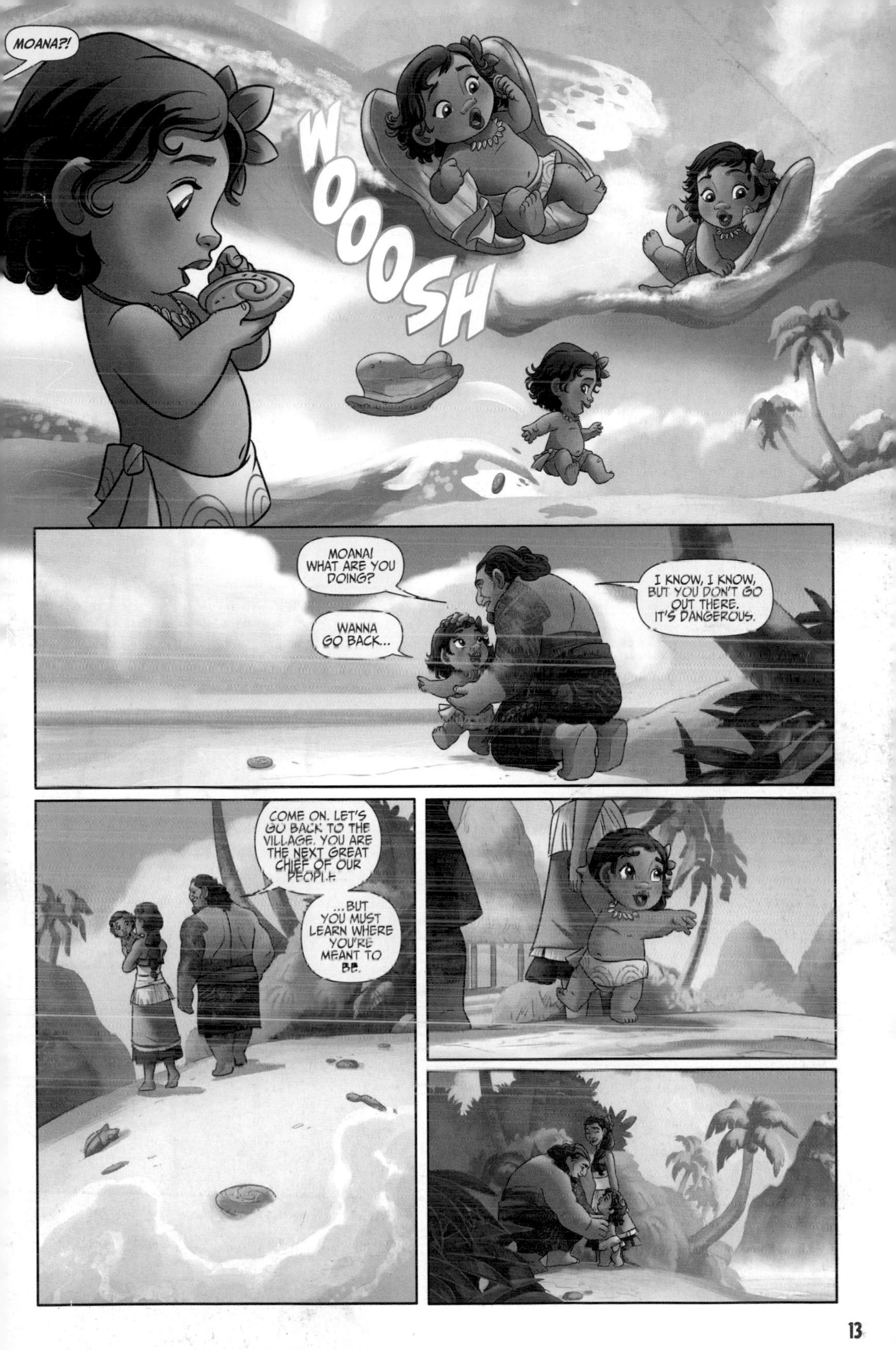

MOANA?!
WOOOOSH
MOANA! WHAT ARE YOU DOING?
WANNA GO BACK...
I KNOW, I KNOW, BUT YOU DON'T GO OUT THERE. IT'S DANGEROUS.
COME ON. LET'S GO BACK TO THE VILLAGE. YOU ARE THE NEXT GREAT CHIEF OF OUR PEOPLE...
...BUT YOU MUST LEARN WHERE YOU'RE MEANT TO BE.

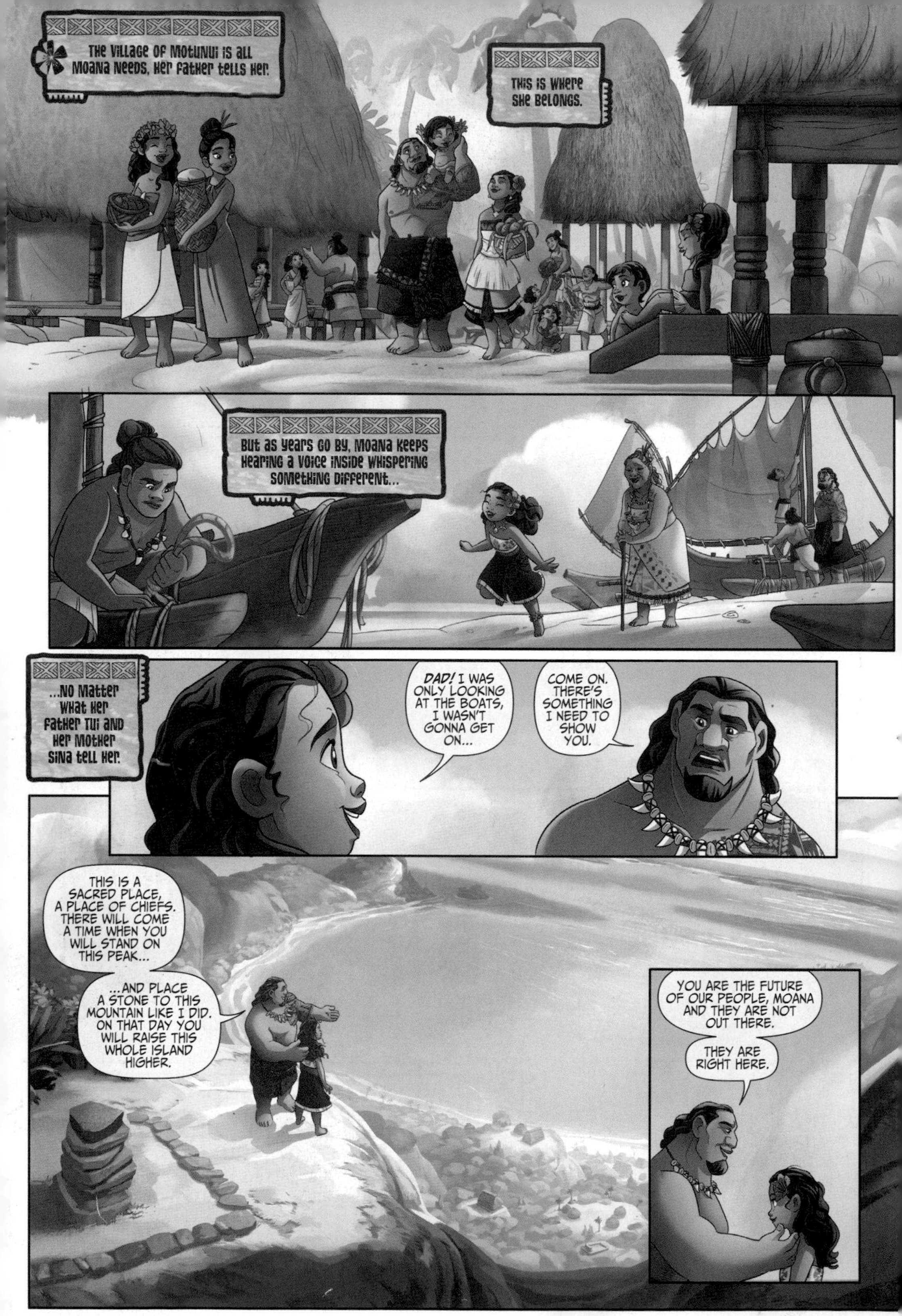
The Village of Motunui is all Moana needs, her father tells her.
This is where she belongs.
But as years go by, Moana keeps hearing a voice inside whispering something different...
...no matter what her father Tui and her mother Sina tell her.
DAD! I WAS ONLY LOOKING AT THE BOATS, I WASN'T GONNA GET ON...
COME ON. THERE'S SOMETHING I NEED TO SHOW YOU.
THIS IS A SACRED PLACE, A PLACE OF CHIEFS. THERE WILL COME A TIME WHEN YOU WILL STAND ON THIS PEAK...
...AND PLACE A STONE TO THIS MOUNTAIN LIKE I DID. ON THAT DAY YOU WILL RAISE THIS WHOLE ISLAND HIGHER.
YOU ARE THE FUTURE OF OUR PEOPLE, MOANA AND THEY ARE NOT OUT THERE.
THEY ARE RIGHT HERE.

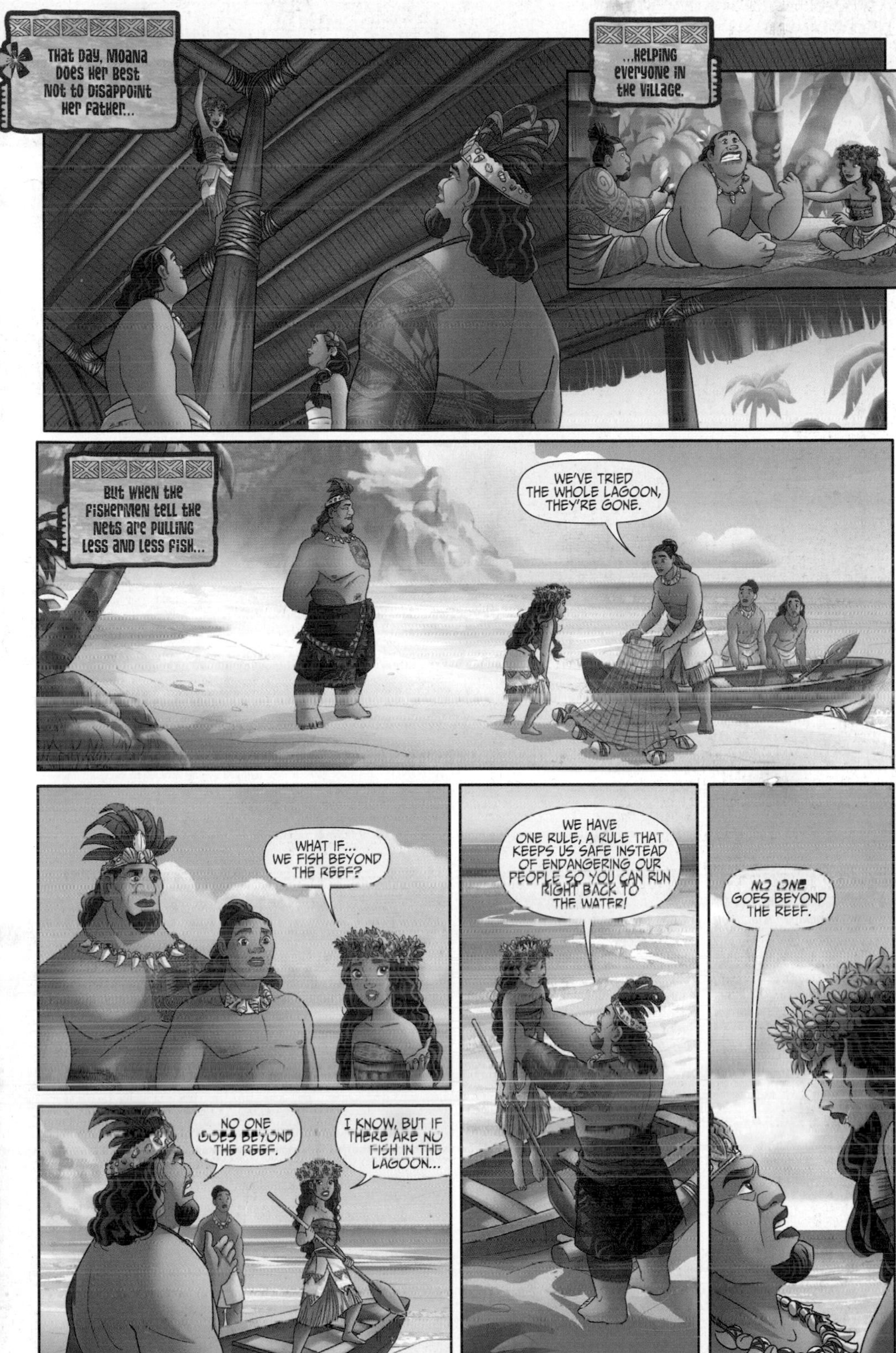
That day, Moana does her best not to disappoint her father...
...helping everyone in the village.
But when the fishermen tell the nets are pulling less and less fish...
WE'VE TRIED THE WHOLE LAGOON, THEY'RE GONE.
WHAT IF... WE FISH BEYOND THE REEF?
NO ONE GOES BEYOND THE REEF.
I KNOW, BUT IF THERE ARE NO FISH IN THE LAGOON...
WE HAVE ONE RULE, A RULE THAT KEEPS US SAFE INSTEAD OF ENDANGERING OUR PEOPLE SO YOU CAN RUN RIGHT BACK TO THE WATER!
NO ONE GOES BEYOND THE REEF.

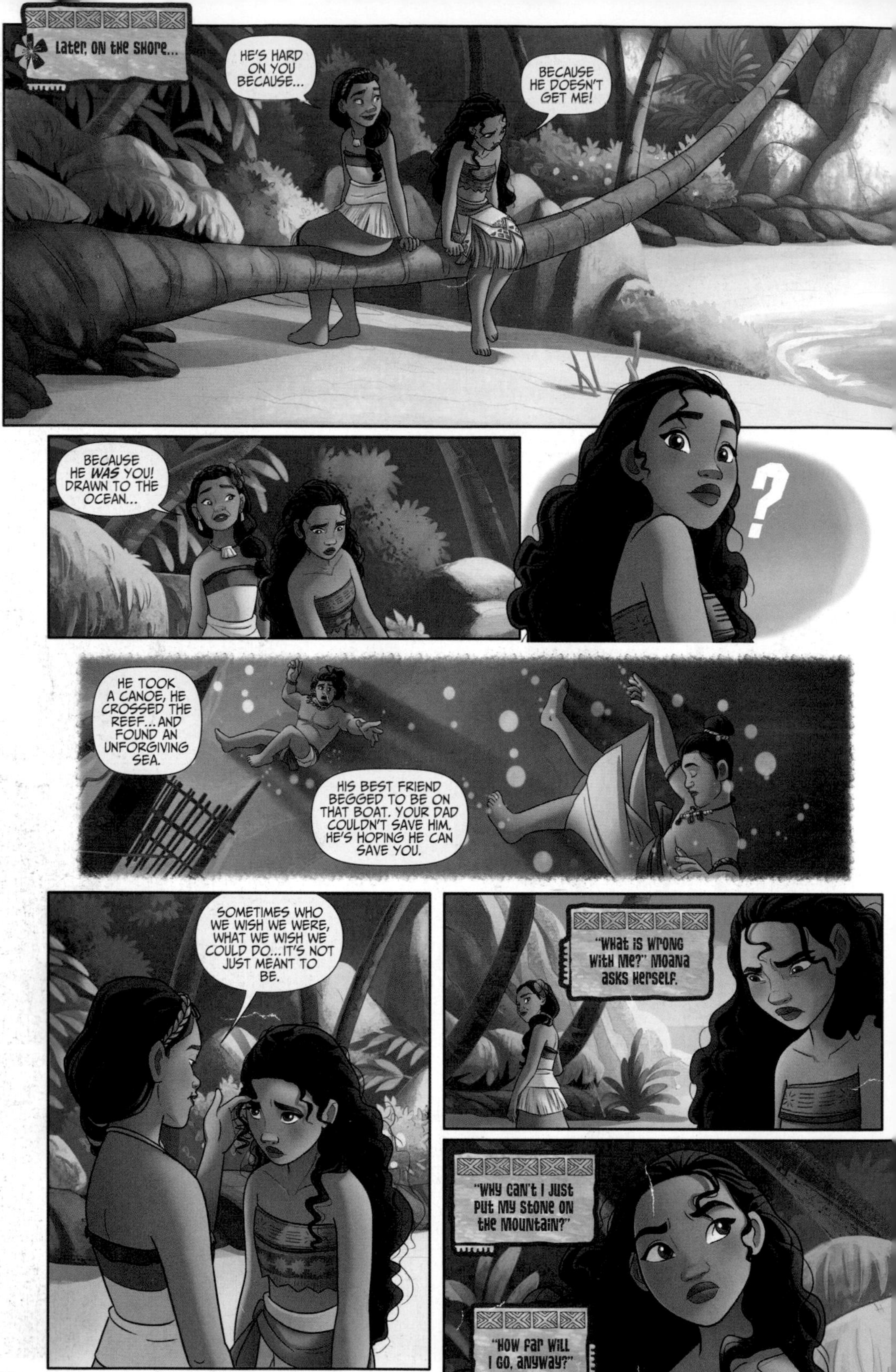

Later, on the shore...
HE'S HARD ON YOU BECAUSE...
BECAUSE HE DOESN'T GET ME!
BECAUSE HE WAS YOU! DRAWN TO THE OCEAN...
?
HE TOOK A CANOE, HE CROSSED THE REEF...AND FOUND AN UNFORGIVING SEA.
HIS BEST FRIEND BEGGED TO BE ON THAT BOAT. YOUR DAD COULDN'T SAVE HIM. HE'S HOPING HE CAN SAVE YOU.
SOMETIMES WHO WE WISH WE WERE, WHAT WE WISH WE COULD DO...IT'S NOT JUST MEANT TO BE.
"What is wrong with me?" Moana asks herself.
"Why can't I just put my stone on the Mountain?"
"How far will I go, anyway?"

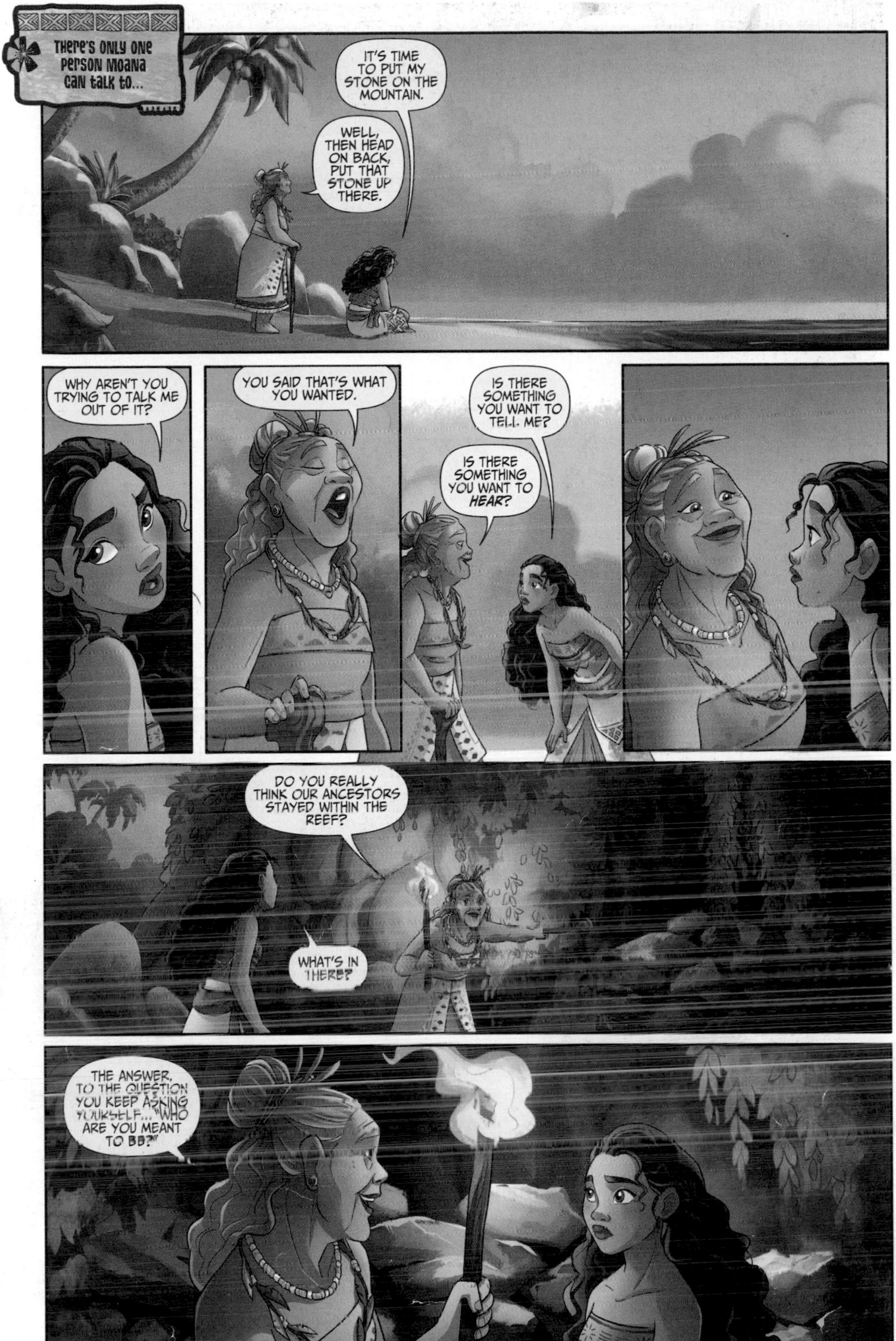
There's only one person Moana can talk to...
IT'S TIME TO PUT MY STONE ON THE MOUNTAIN.
WELL, THEN HEAD ON BACK, PUT THAT STONE UP THERE.
WHY AREN'T YOU TRYING TO TALK ME OUT OF IT?
YOU SAID THAT'S WHAT YOU WANTED.
IS THERE SOMETHING YOU WANT TO TELL ME?
IS THERE SOMETHING YOU WANT TO *HEAR?*
DO YOU REALLY THINK OUR ANCESTORS STAYED WITHIN THE REEF?
WHAT'S IN THERE?
THE ANSWER, TO THE QUESTION YOU KEEP ASKING YOURSELF... "WHO ARE YOU MEANT TO BE?"

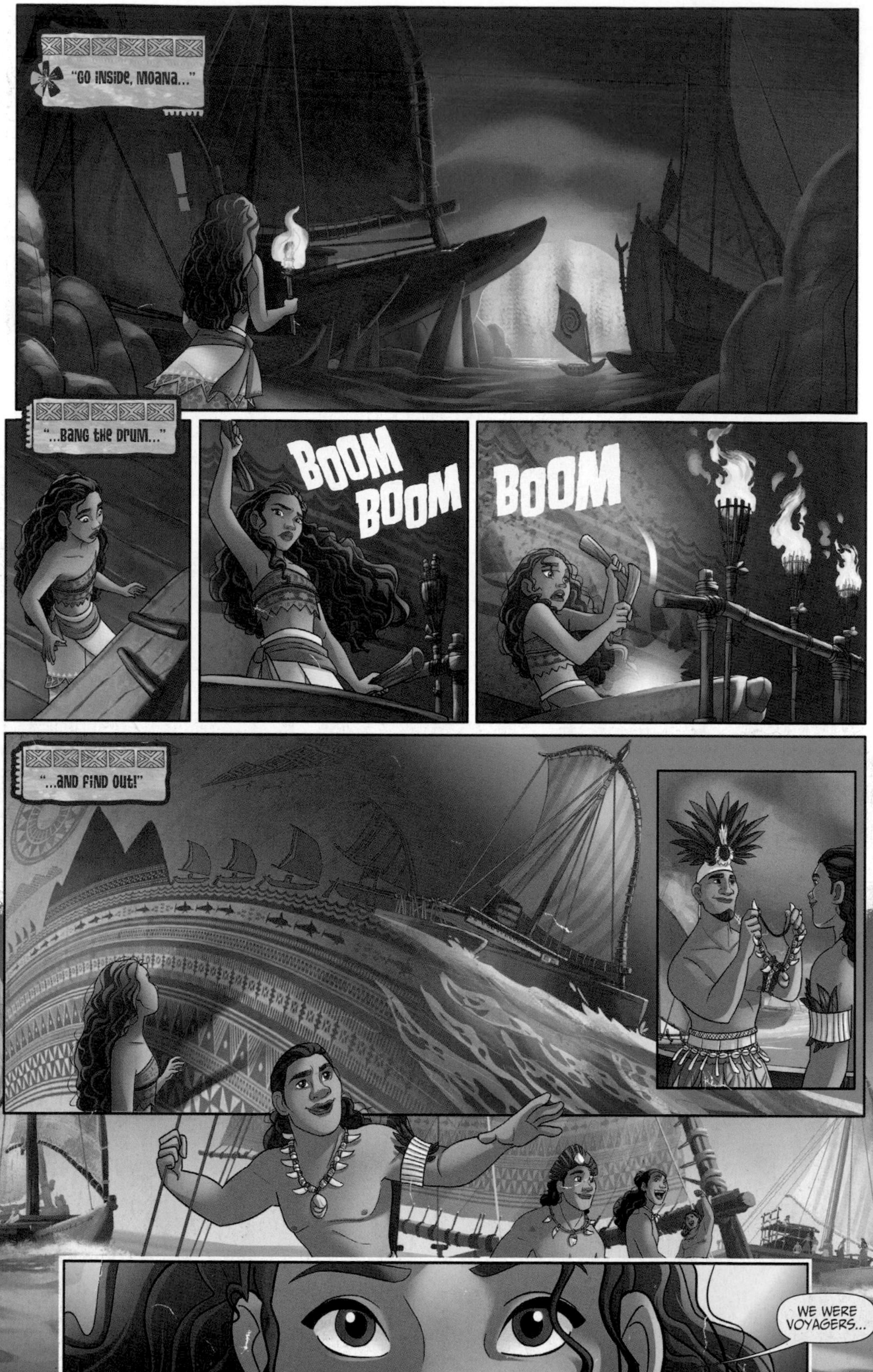
"GO INSIDE, MOANA..."
"...BANG THE DRUM..."
BOOM
BOOM
BOOM
"...AND FIND OUT!"
WE WERE VOYAGERS...

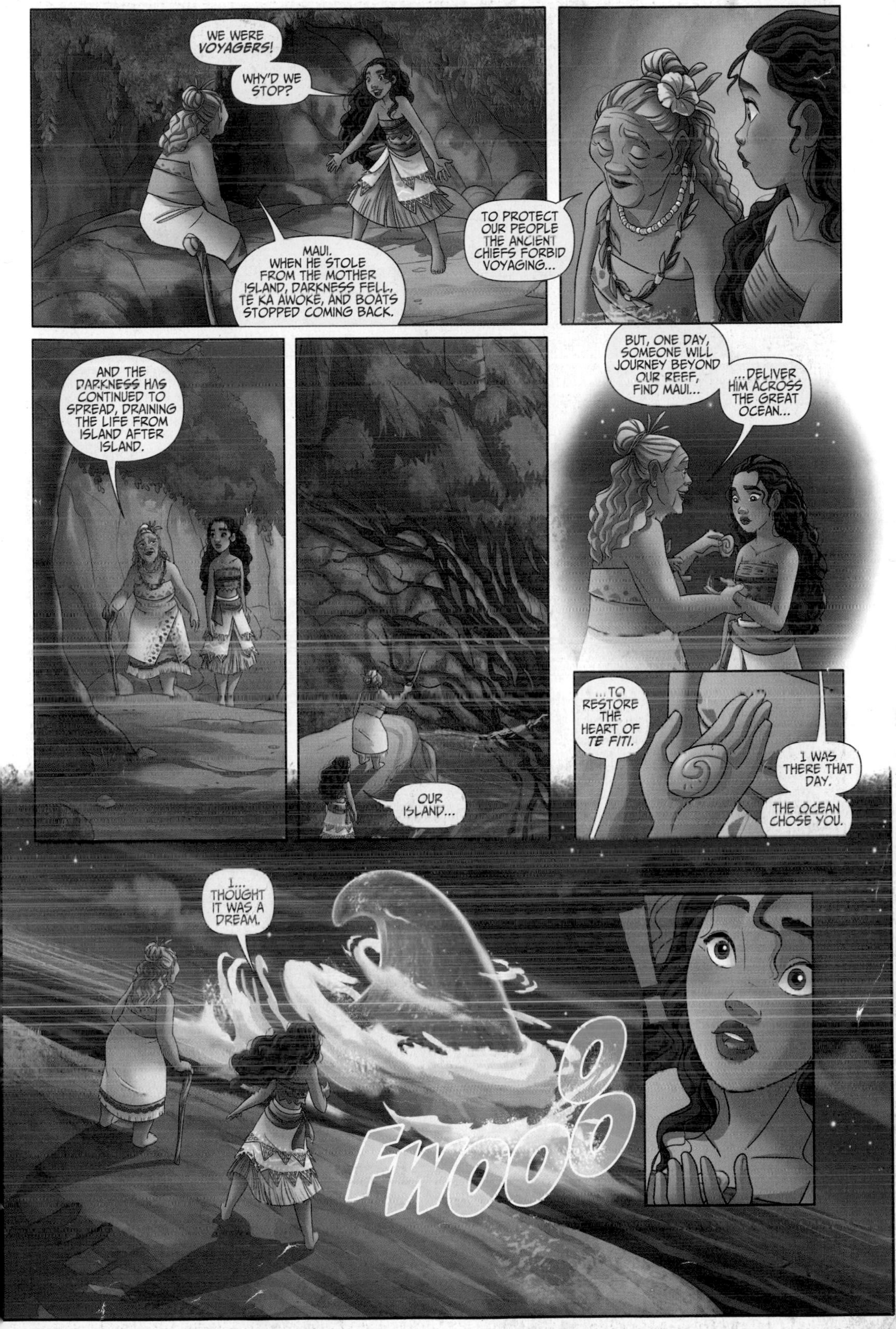
WE WERE VOYAGERS!
WHY'D WE STOP?
MAUI. WHEN HE STOLE FROM THE MOTHER ISLAND, DARKNESS FELL, TE KA AWOKE, AND BOATS STOPPED COMING BACK.
TO PROTECT OUR PEOPLE THE ANCIENT CHIEFS FORBID VOYAGING...
AND THE DARKNESS HAS CONTINUED TO SPREAD, DRAINING THE LIFE FROM ISLAND AFTER ISLAND.
OUR ISLAND...
BUT, ONE DAY, SOMEONE WILL JOURNEY BEYOND OUR REEF, FIND MAUI...
...DELIVER HIM ACROSS THE GREAT OCEAN...
...TO RESTORE THE HEART OF TE FITI.
I WAS THERE THAT DAY.
THE OCEAN CHOSE YOU.
I... THOUGHT IT WAS A DREAM.
FWOOOO

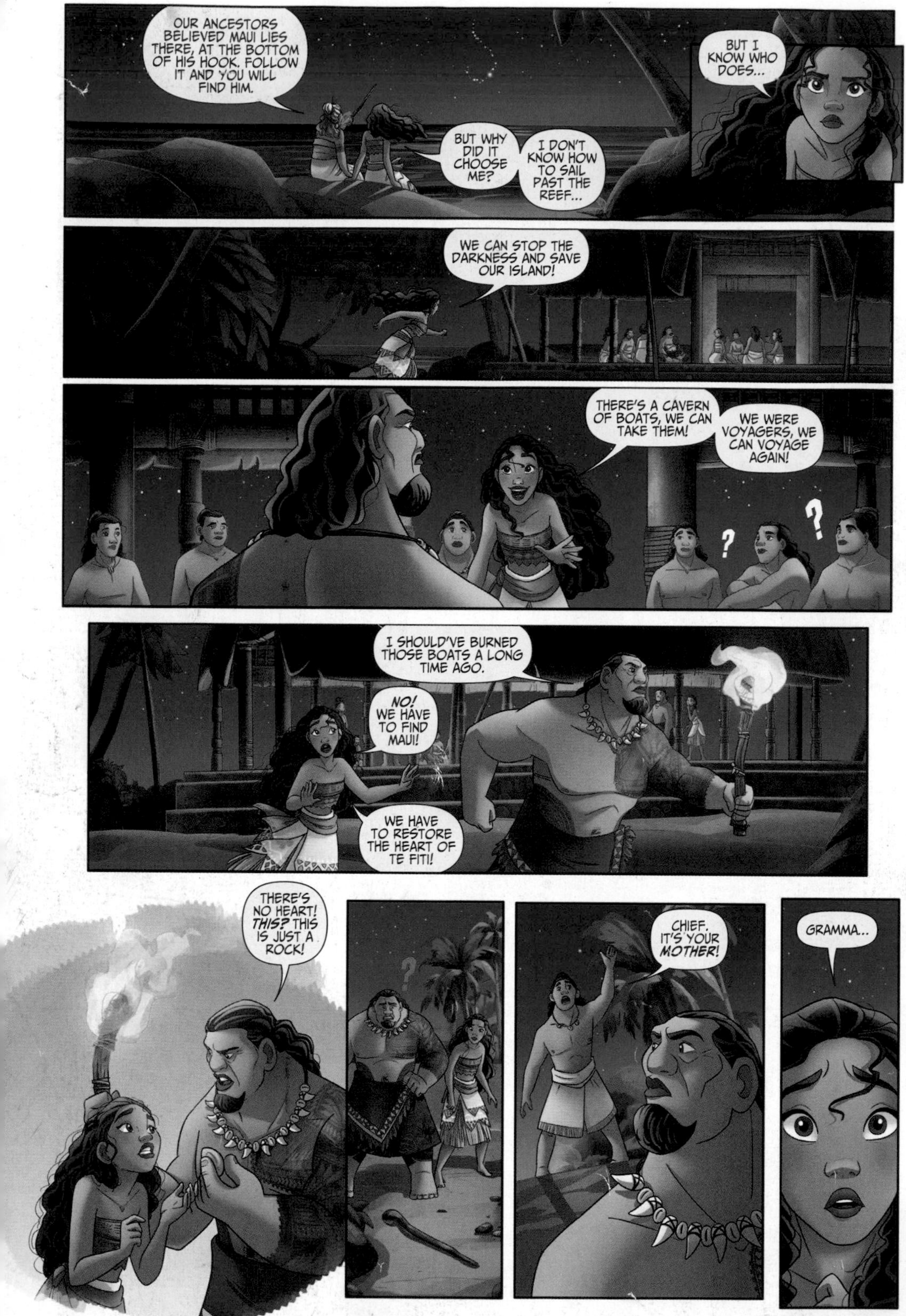
OUR ANCESTORS BELIEVED MAUI LIES THERE, AT THE BOTTOM OF HIS HOOK. FOLLOW IT AND YOU WILL FIND HIM.
BUT WHY DID IT CHOOSE ME?
I DON'T KNOW HOW TO SAIL PAST THE REEF...
BUT I KNOW WHO DOES...
WE CAN STOP THE DARKNESS AND SAVE OUR ISLAND!
THERE'S A CAVERN OF BOATS, WE CAN TAKE THEM!
WE WERE VOYAGERS, WE CAN VOYAGE AGAIN!
?
?
I SHOULD'VE BURNED THOSE BOATS A LONG TIME AGO.
NO! WE HAVE TO FIND MAUI!
WE HAVE TO RESTORE THE HEART OF TE FITI!
THERE'S NO HEART! *THIS?* THIS IS JUST A ROCK!
?
CHIEF. IT'S YOUR *MOTHER*!
GRAMMA...

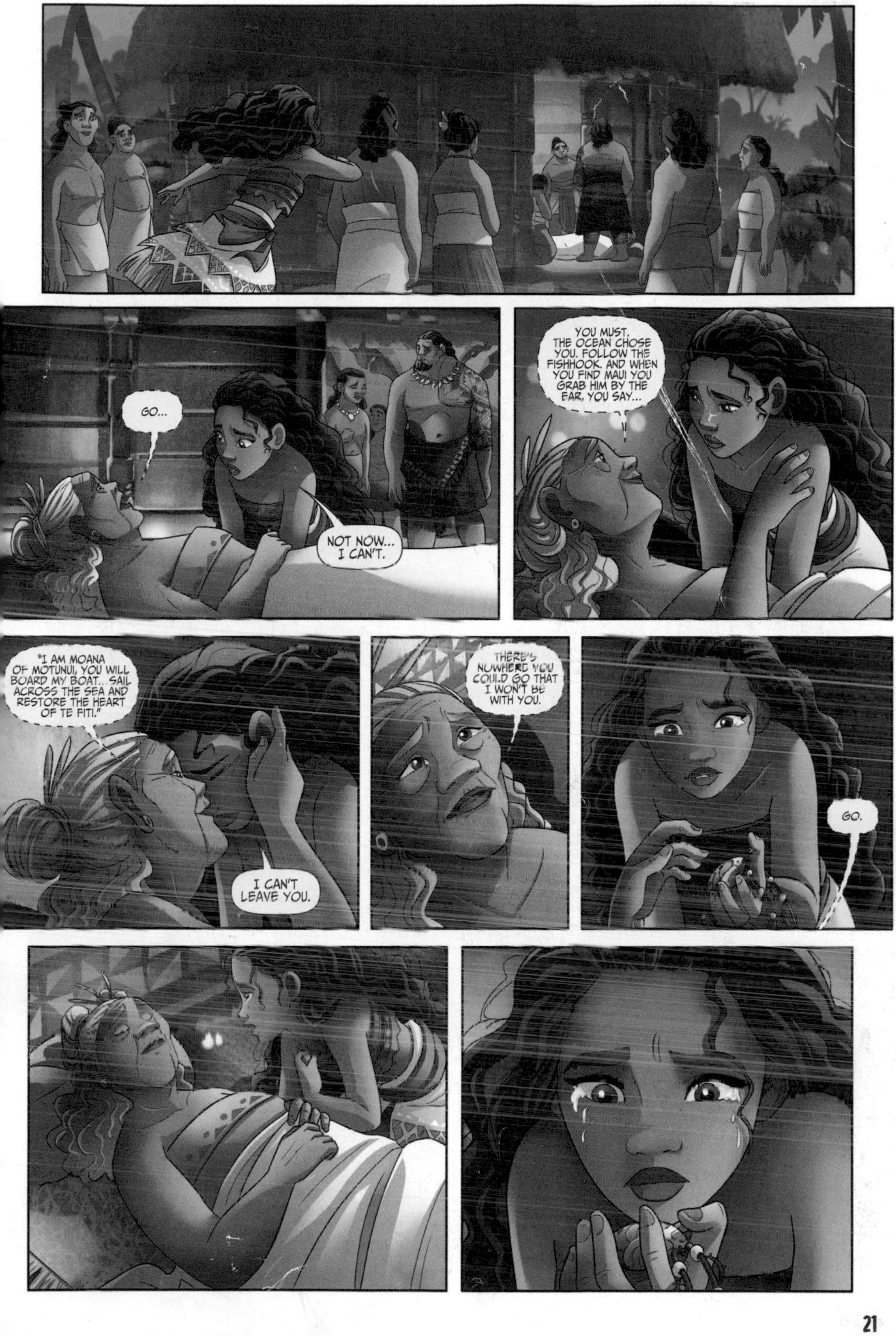
GO...
NOT NOW... I CAN'T.
YOU MUST. THE OCEAN CHOSE YOU. FOLLOW THE FISHHOOK. AND WHEN YOU FIND MAUI YOU GRAB HIM BY THE EAR, YOU SAY...
"I AM MOANA OF MOTUNUI, YOU WILL BOARD MY BOAT... SAIL ACROSS THE SEA AND RESTORE THE HEART OF TE FITI."
I CAN'T LEAVE YOU.
THERE'S NOWHERE YOU COULD GO THAT I WON'T BE WITH YOU.
GO.

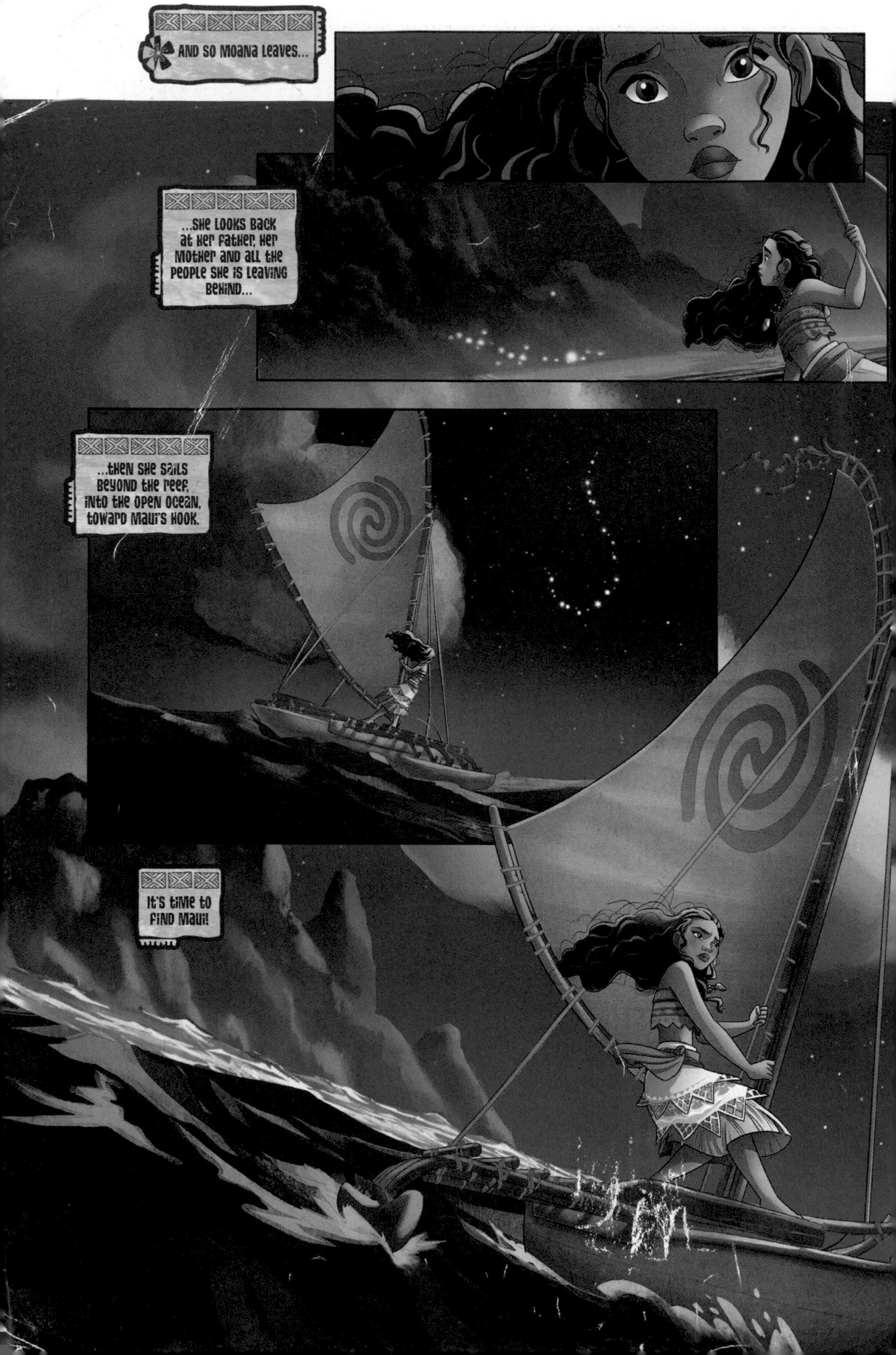
AND SO MOANA LEAVES...
...SHE LOOKS BACK AT HER FATHER, HER MOTHER AND ALL THE PEOPLE SHE IS LEAVING BEHIND...
...THEN SHE SAILS BEYOND THE REEF, INTO THE OPEN OCEAN, TOWARD MAUI'S HOOK.
IT'S TIME TO FIND MAUI!

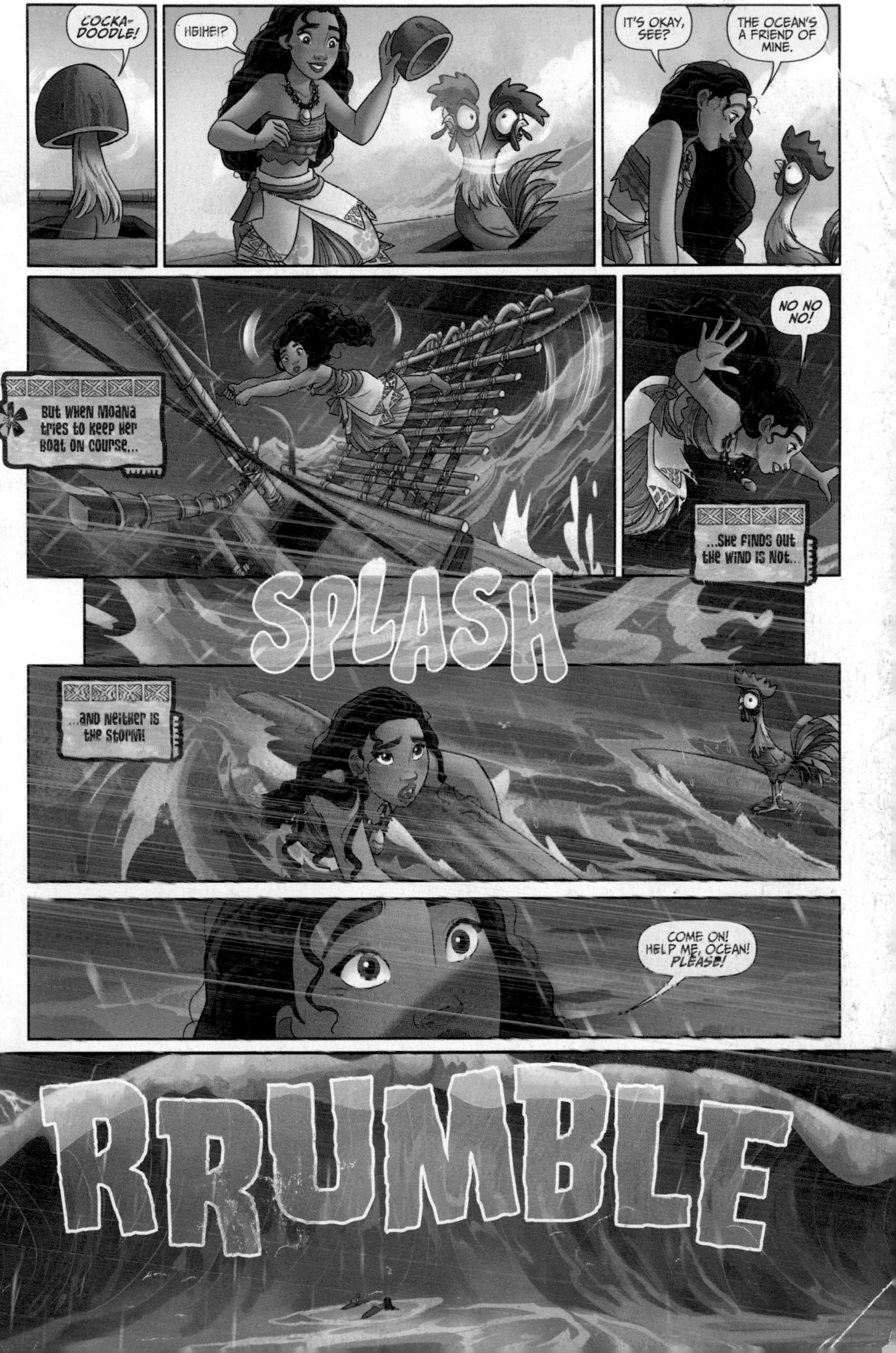
COCKA-DOODLE!
HEIHEI?
IT'S OKAY, SEE?
THE OCEAN'S A FRIEND OF MINE.
But when Moana tries to keep her boat on course...
NO NO NO!
...she finds out the wind is not...
SPLASH
...and neither is the storm!
COME ON! HELP ME, OCEAN! PLEASE!
RRUMBLE

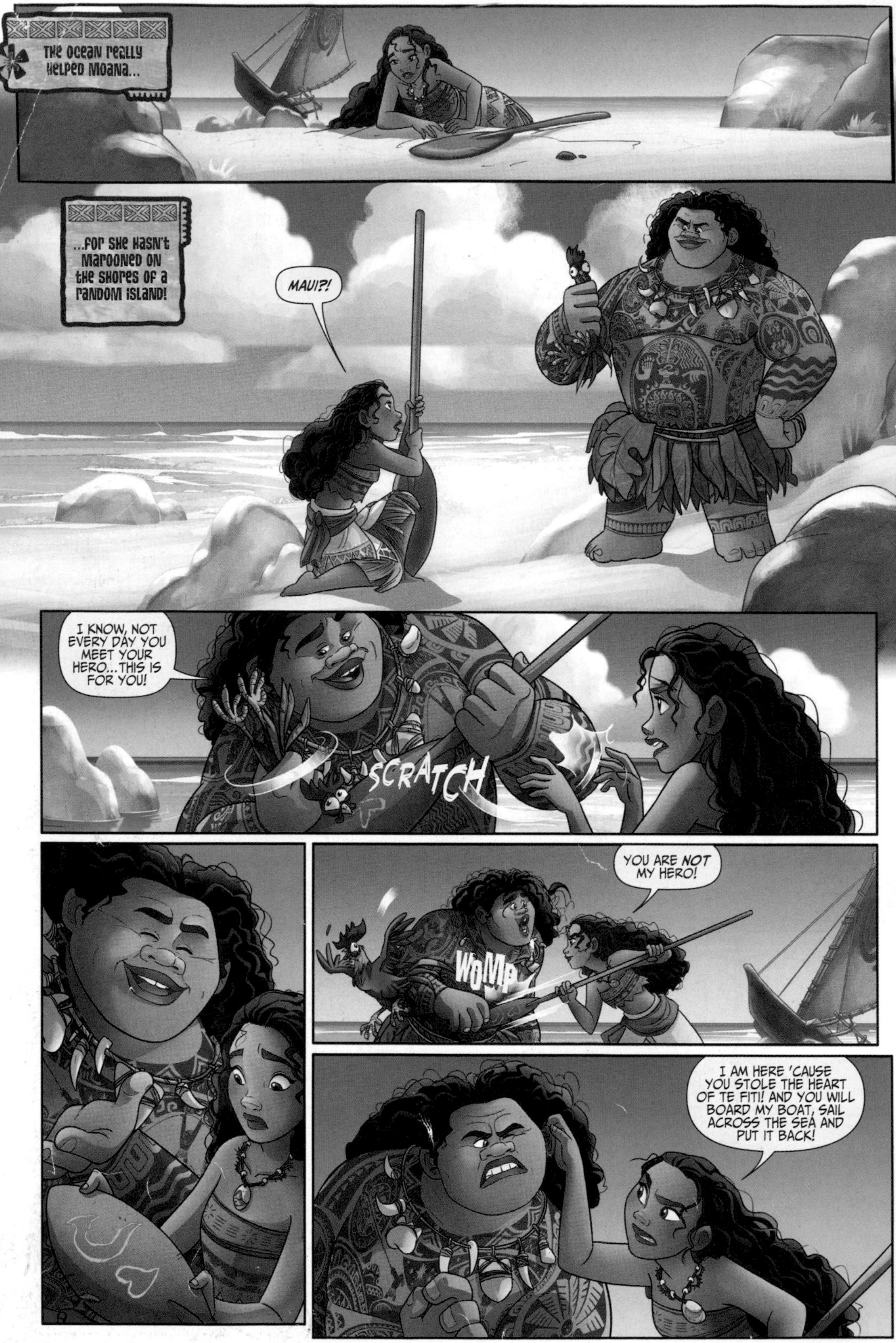
The ocean really helped Moana...
...for she hasn't marooned on the shores of a random island!
MAUI?!
I KNOW, NOT EVERY DAY YOU MEET YOUR HERO...THIS IS FOR YOU!
SCRATCH
YOU ARE NOT MY HERO!
WOMP
I AM HERE 'CAUSE YOU STOLE THE HEART OF TE FITI! AND YOU WILL BOARD MY BOAT, SAIL ACROSS THE SEA AND PUT IT BACK!

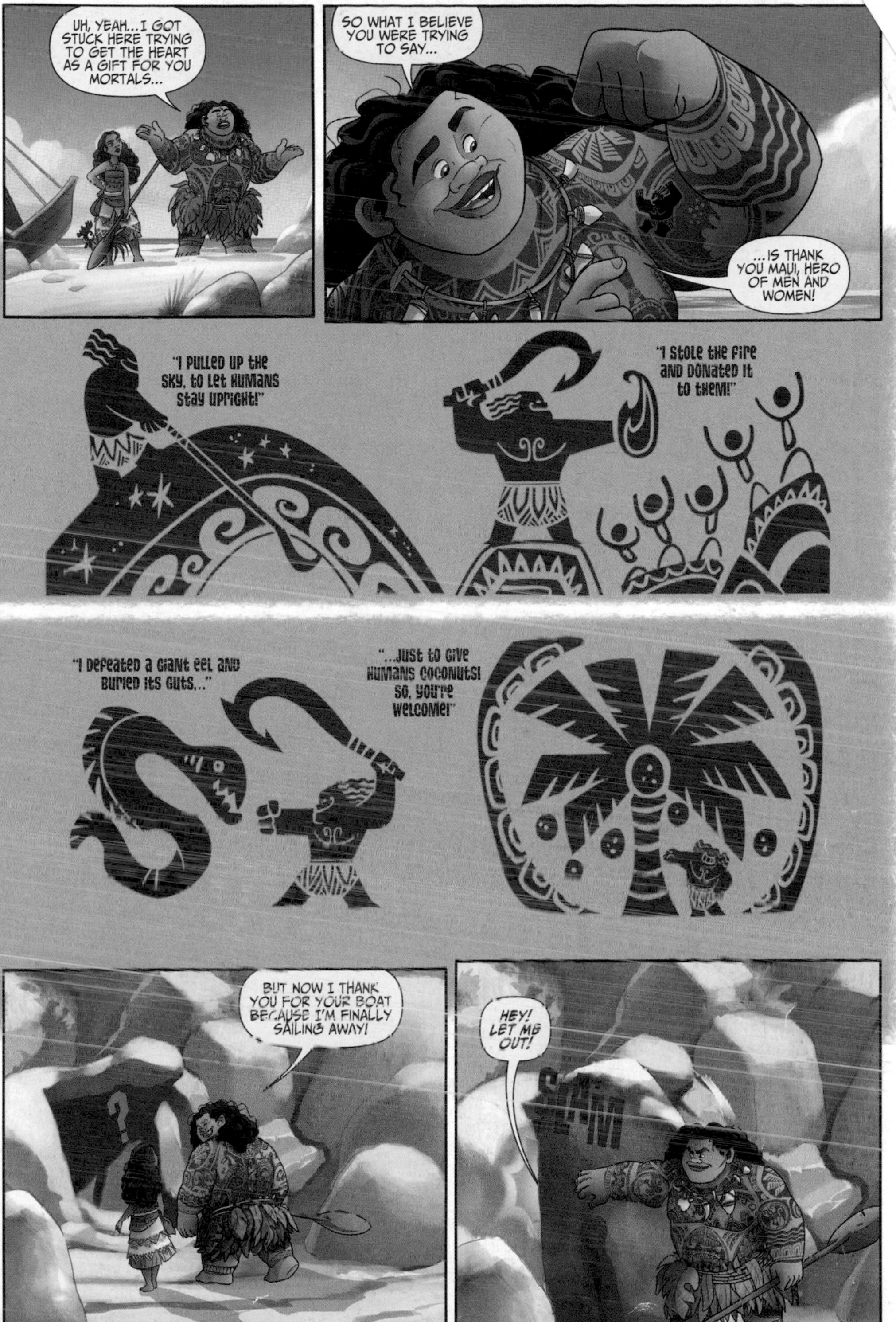
UH, YEAH... I GOT STUCK HERE TRYING TO GET THE HEART AS A GIFT FOR YOU MORTALS...
SO WHAT I BELIEVE YOU WERE TRYING TO SAY...
...IS THANK YOU MAUI, HERO OF MEN AND WOMEN!
"I PULLED UP THE SKY, TO LET HUMANS STAY UPRIGHT!"
"I STOLE THE FIRE AND DONATED IT TO THEM!"
"I DEFEATED A GIANT EEL AND BURIED ITS GUTS..."
"...JUST TO GIVE HUMANS COCONUTS! SO, YOU'RE WELCOME!"
BUT NOW I THANK YOU FOR YOUR BOAT BECAUSE I'M FINALLY SAILING AWAY!
?
HEY! LET ME OUT!
SLAM

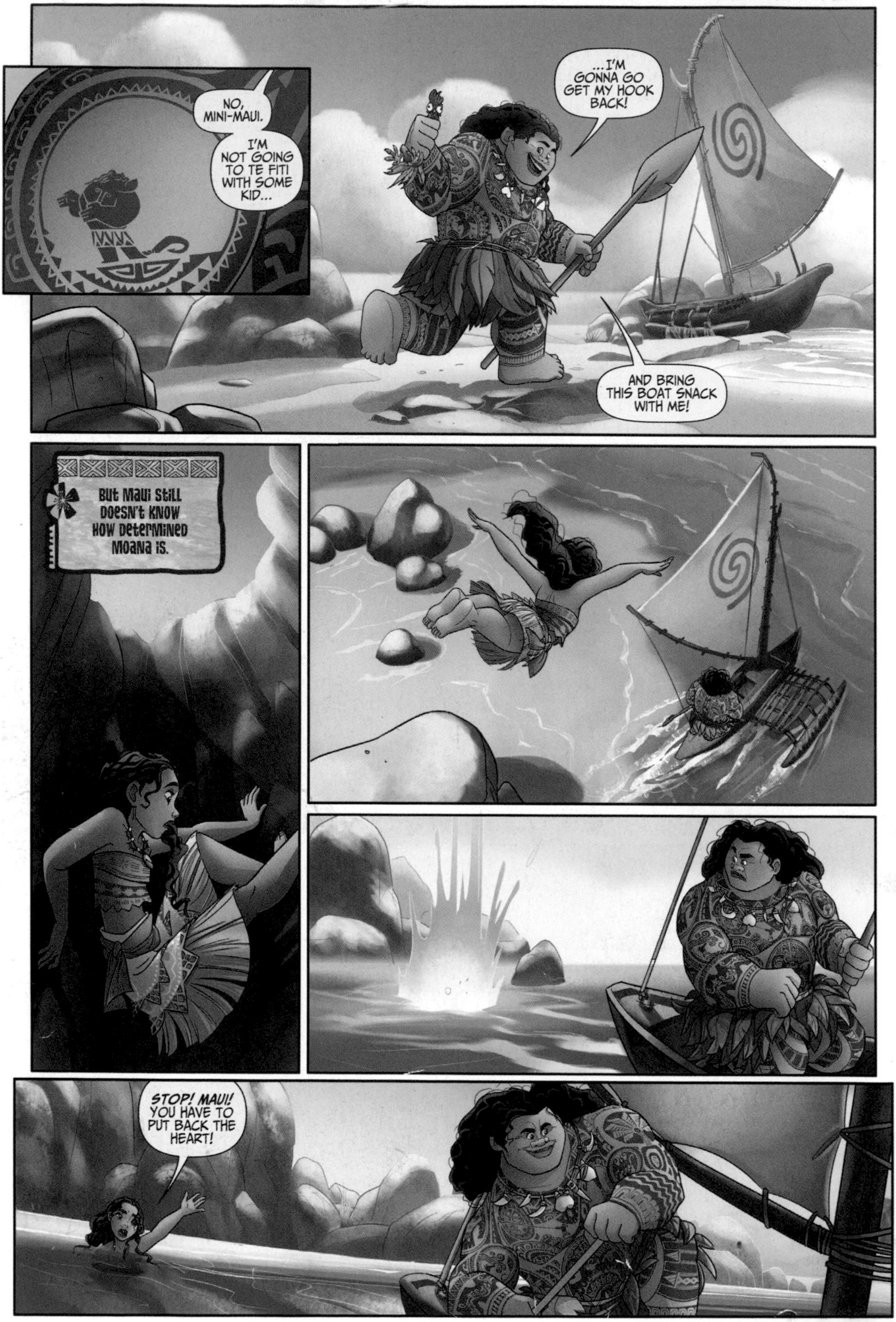
NO, MINI-MAUI.
I'M NOT GOING TO TE FITI WITH SOME KID...
...I'M GONNA GO GET MY HOOK BACK!
AND BRING THIS BOAT SNACK WITH ME!
But Maui still doesn't know how determined Moana is.
STOP! MAUI! YOU HAVE TO PUT BACK THE HEART!

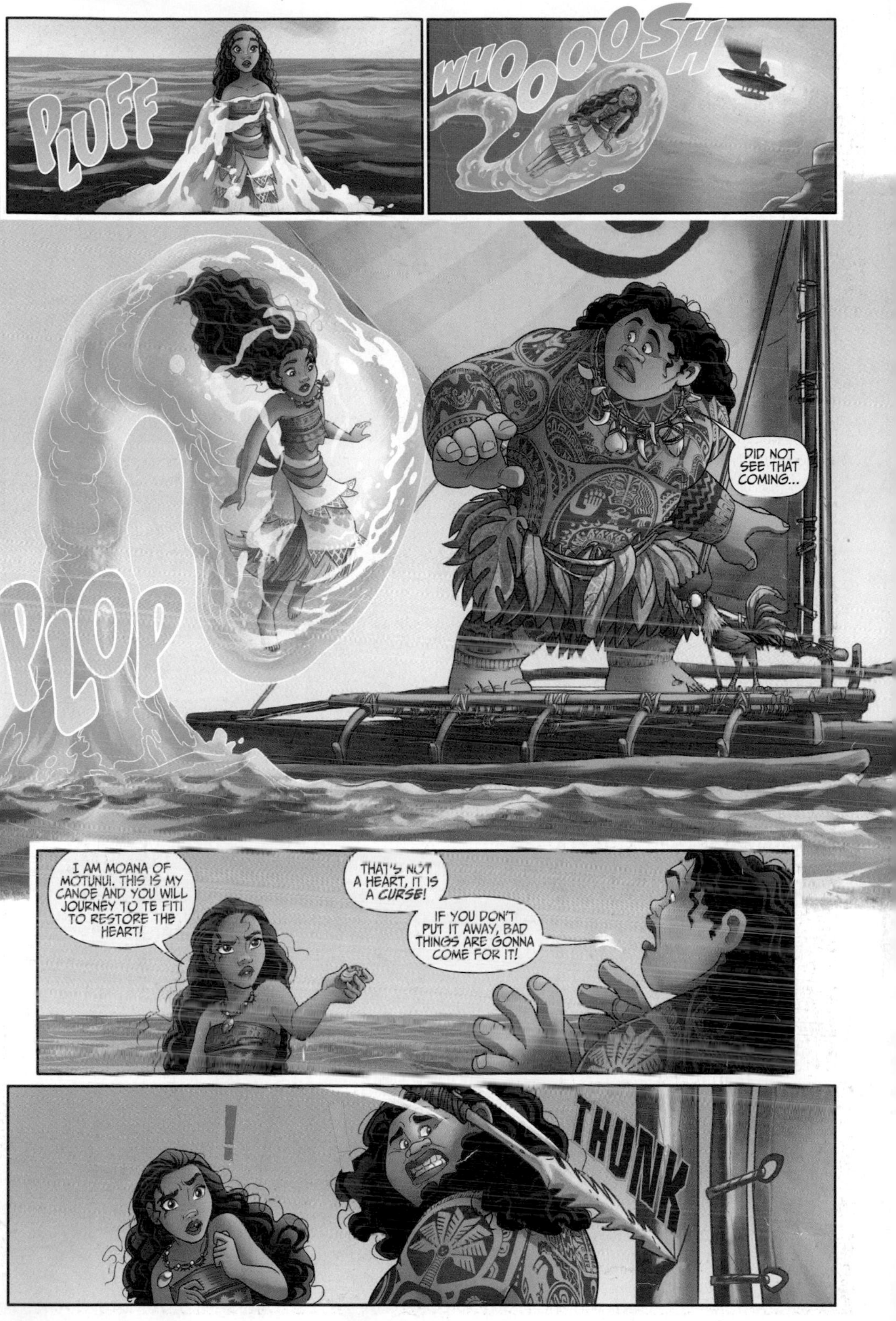
PLUFF
WHOOOOOSH
PLOP
DID NOT SEE THAT COMING...
I AM MOANA OF MOTUNUI. THIS IS MY CANOE AND YOU WILL JOURNEY TO TE FITI TO RESTORE THE HEART!
THAT'S NOT A HEART, IT IS A *CURSE*!
IF YOU DON'T PUT IT AWAY, BAD THINGS ARE GONNA COME FOR IT!
!
THUNK

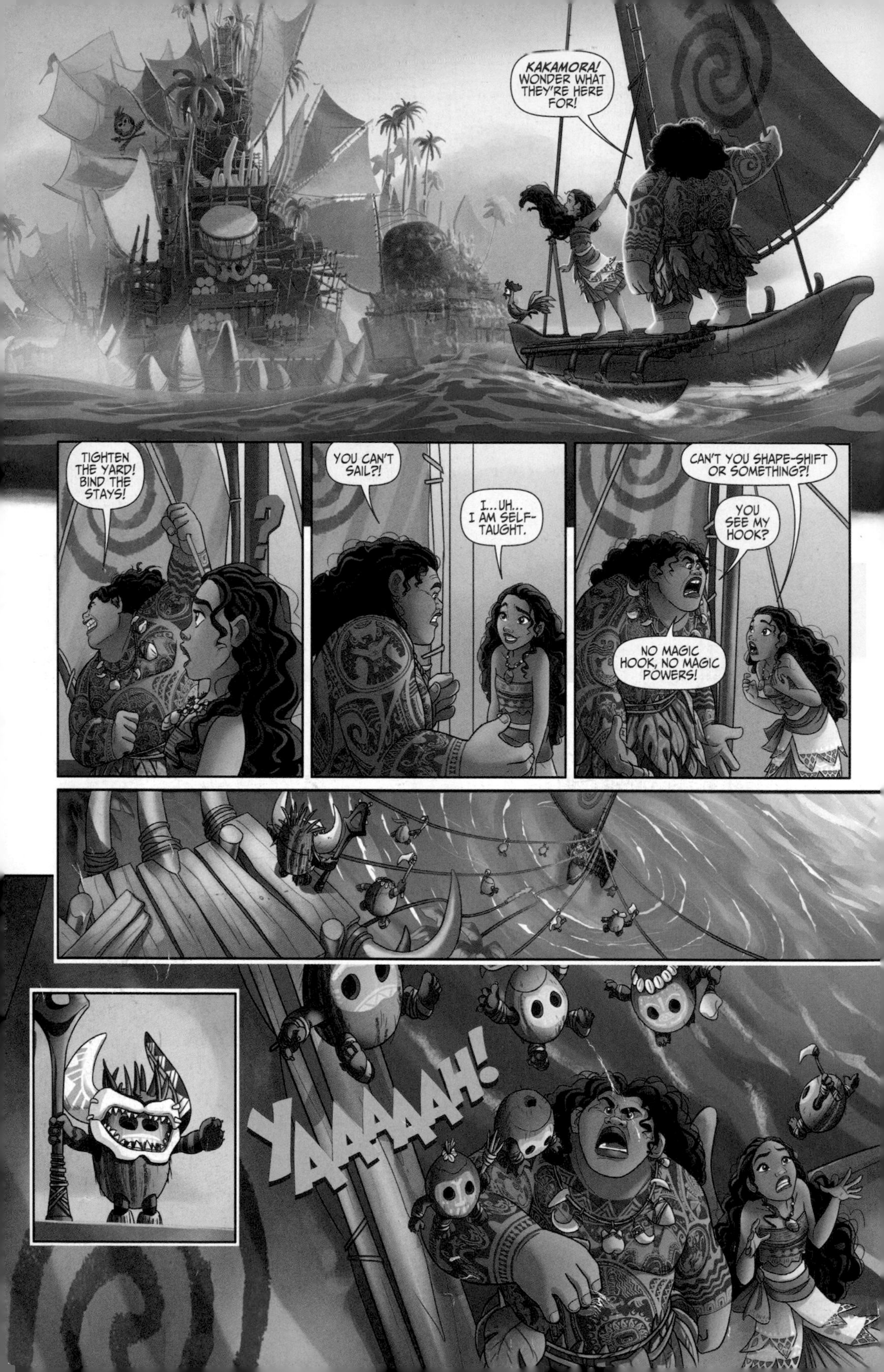
KAKAMORA! WONDER WHAT THEY'RE HERE FOR!
TIGHTEN THE YARD! BIND THE STAYS!
YOU CAN'T SAIL?!
I...UH... I AM SELF-TAUGHT.
CAN'T YOU SHAPE-SHIFT OR SOMETHING?!
YOU SEE MY HOOK?
NO MAGIC HOOK, NO MAGIC POWERS!
YAAAAAH!

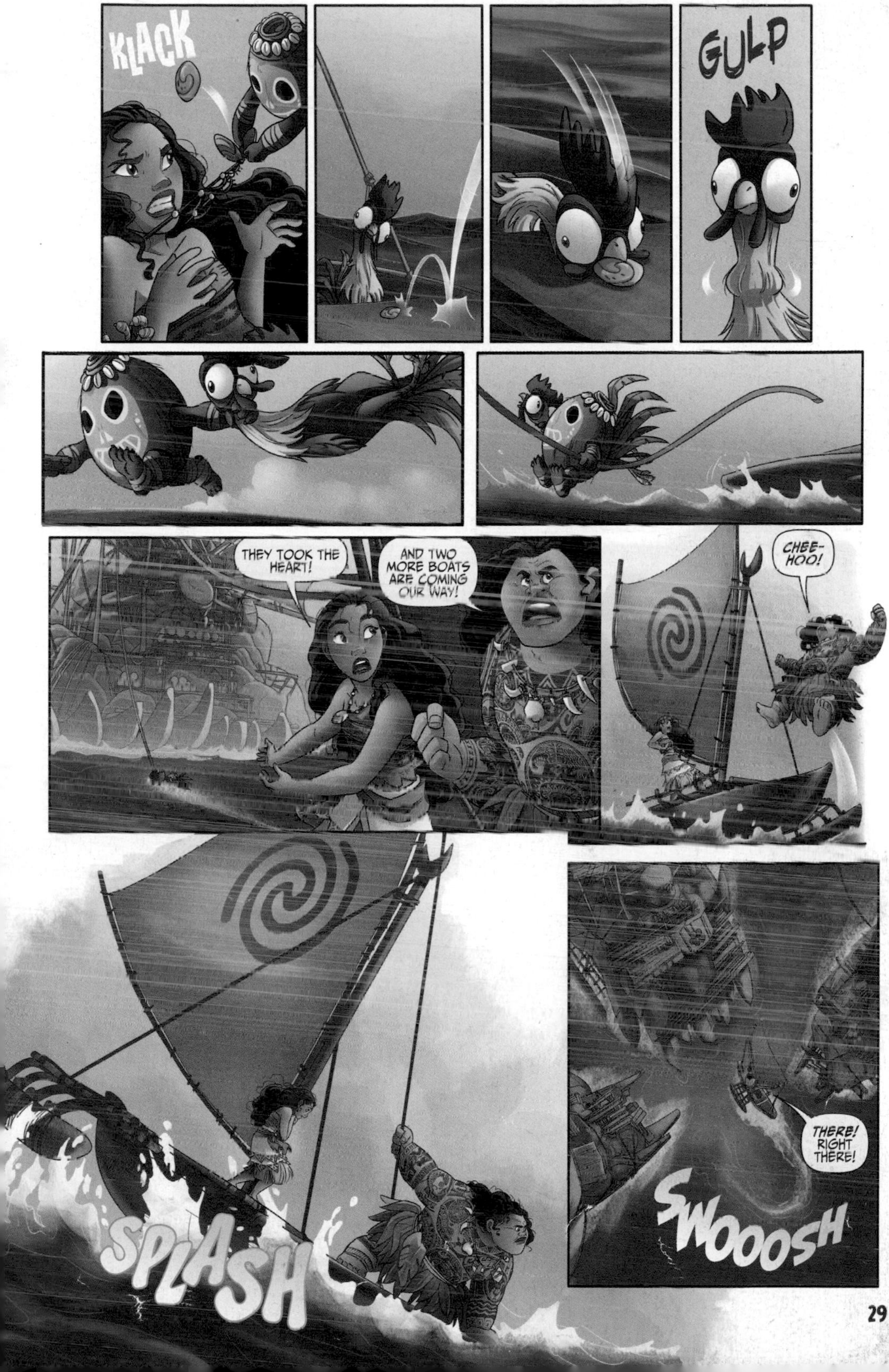
KLACK
GULP
THEY TOOK THE HEART!
AND TWO MORE BOATS ARE COMING OUR WAY!
CHEE-HOO!
SPLASH
THERE! RIGHT THERE!
SWOOOSH

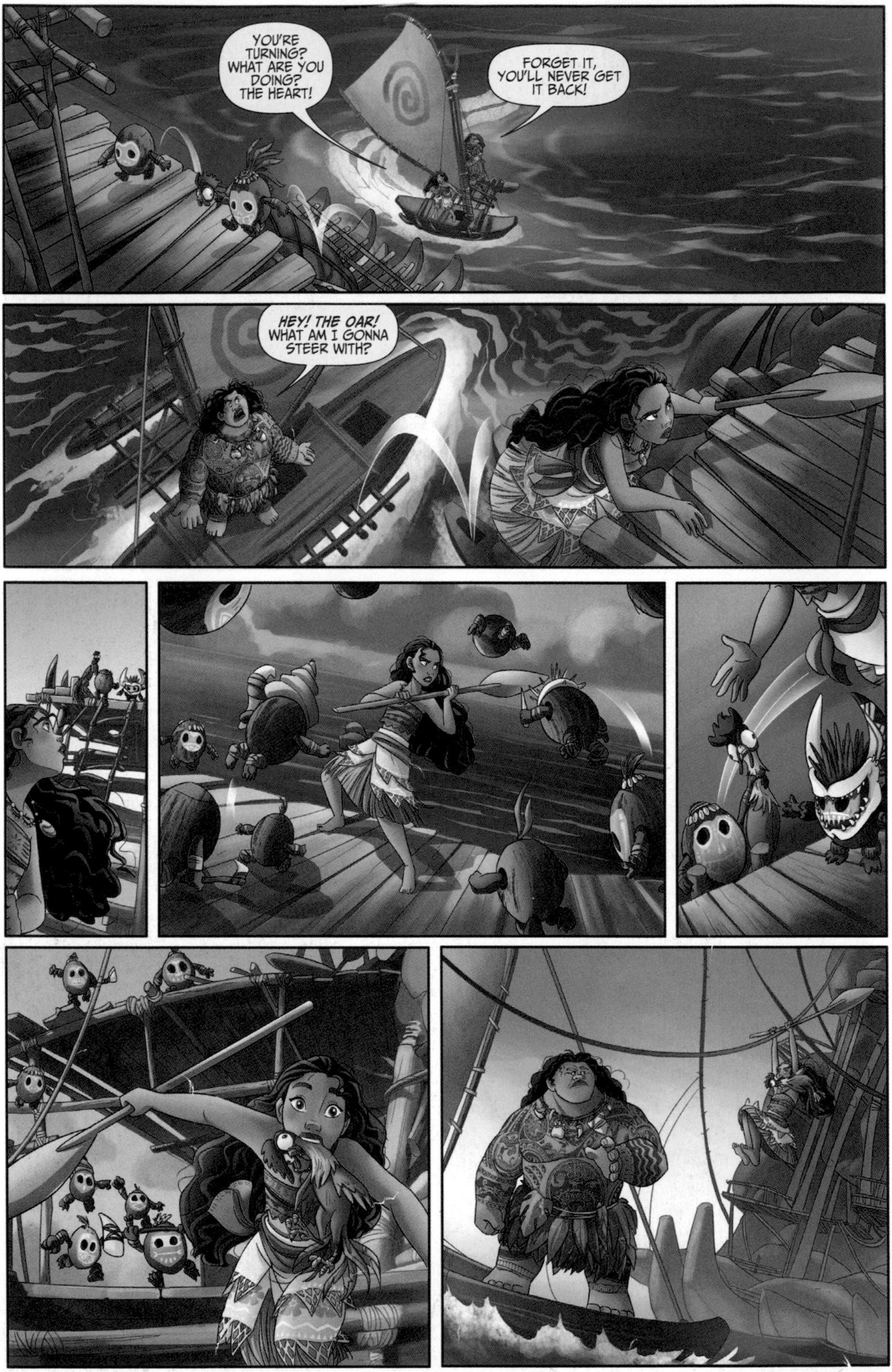
YOU'RE TURNING? WHAT ARE YOU DOING? THE HEART!
FORGET IT, YOU'LL NEVER GET IT BACK!
HEY! THE OAR! WHAT AM I GONNA STEER WITH?

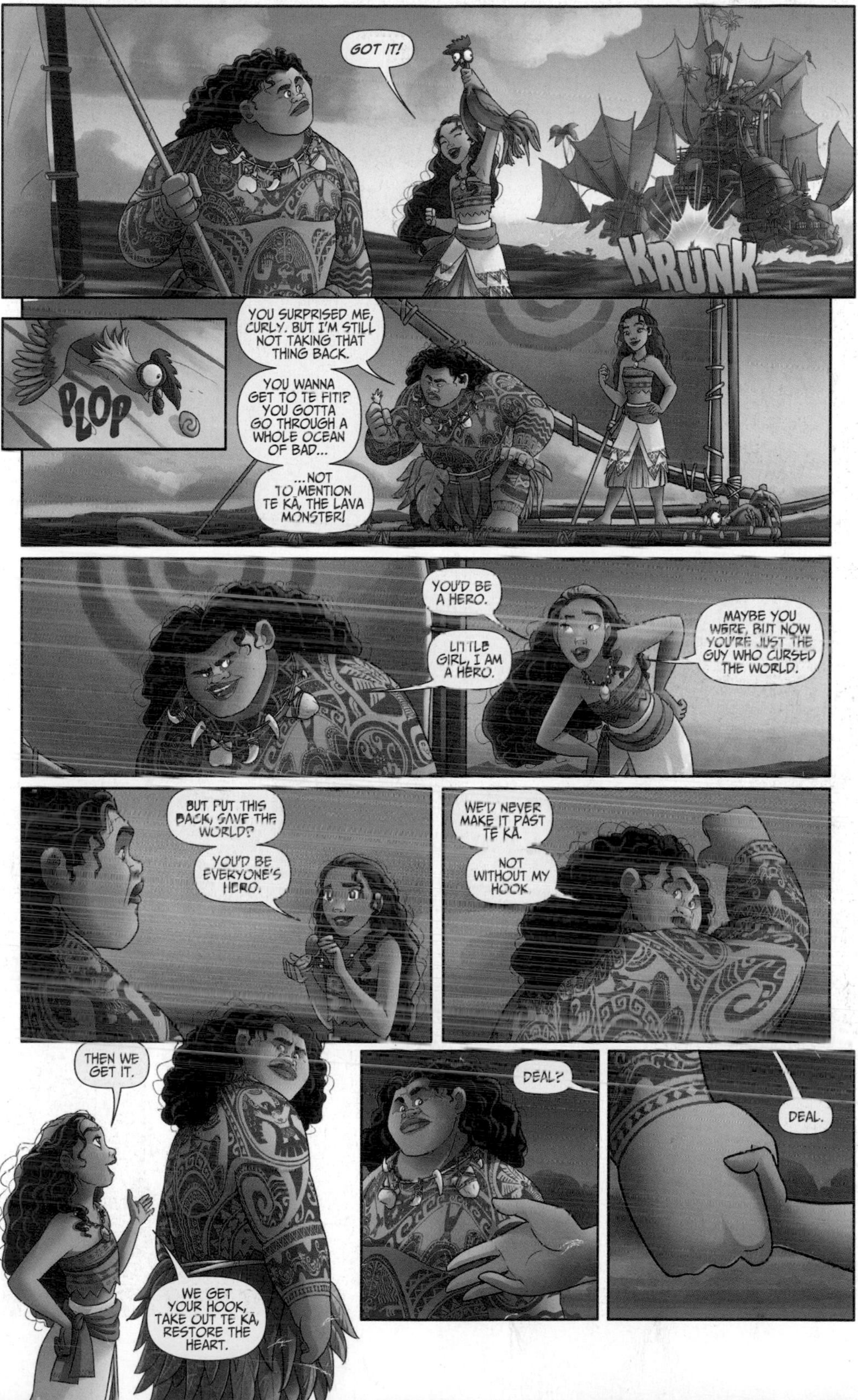
GOT IT!
KRUNK
PLOP
YOU SURPRISED ME, CURLY. BUT I'M STILL NOT TAKING THAT THING BACK.
YOU WANNA GET TO TE FITI? YOU GOTTA GO THROUGH A WHOLE OCEAN OF BAD...
...NOT TO MENTION TE KĀ, THE LAVA MONSTER!
YOU'D BE A HERO.
LITTLE GIRL, I AM A HERO.
MAYBE YOU WERE, BUT NOW YOU'RE JUST THE GUY WHO CURSED THE WORLD.
BUT PUT THIS BACK, SAVE THE WORLD?
YOU'D BE EVERYONE'S HERO.
WE'D NEVER MAKE IT PAST TE KĀ.
NOT WITHOUT MY HOOK.
THEN WE GET IT.
WE GET YOUR HOOK, TAKE OUT TE KĀ, RESTORE THE HEART.
DEAL?
DEAL.

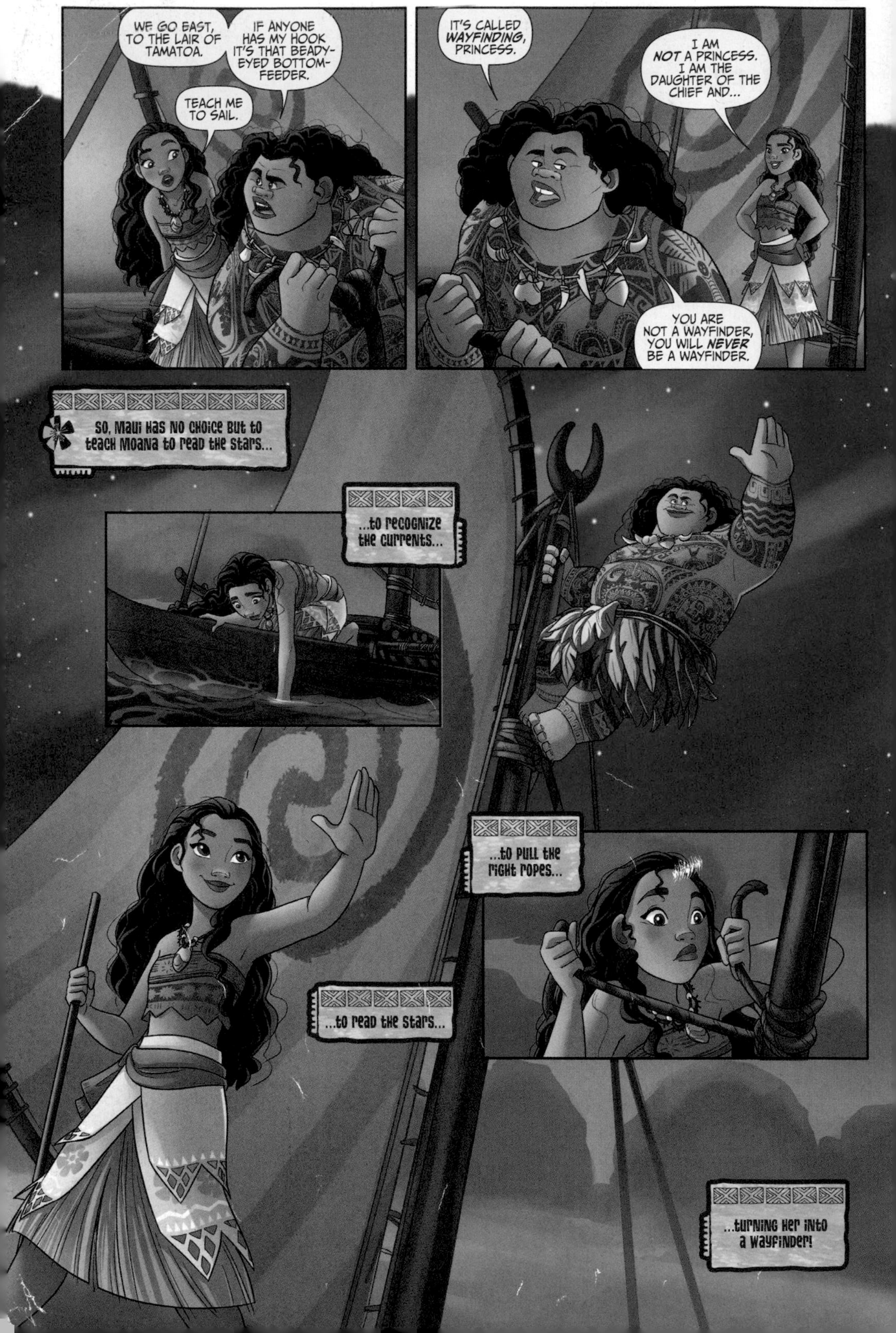

WE GO EAST, TO THE LAIR OF TAMATOA.
IF ANYONE HAS MY HOOK IT'S THAT BEADY-EYED BOTTOM-FEEDER.
TEACH ME TO SAIL.
IT'S CALLED *WAYFINDING*, PRINCESS.
I AM *NOT* A PRINCESS. I AM THE DAUGHTER OF THE CHIEF AND...
YOU ARE NOT A WAYFINDER, YOU WILL *NEVER* BE A WAYFINDER.
SO, MAUI HAS NO CHOICE BUT TO TEACH MOANA TO READ THE STARS...
...TO RECOGNIZE THE CURRENTS...
...TO PULL THE RIGHT ROPES...
...TO READ THE STARS...
...TURNING HER INTO A WAYFINDER!

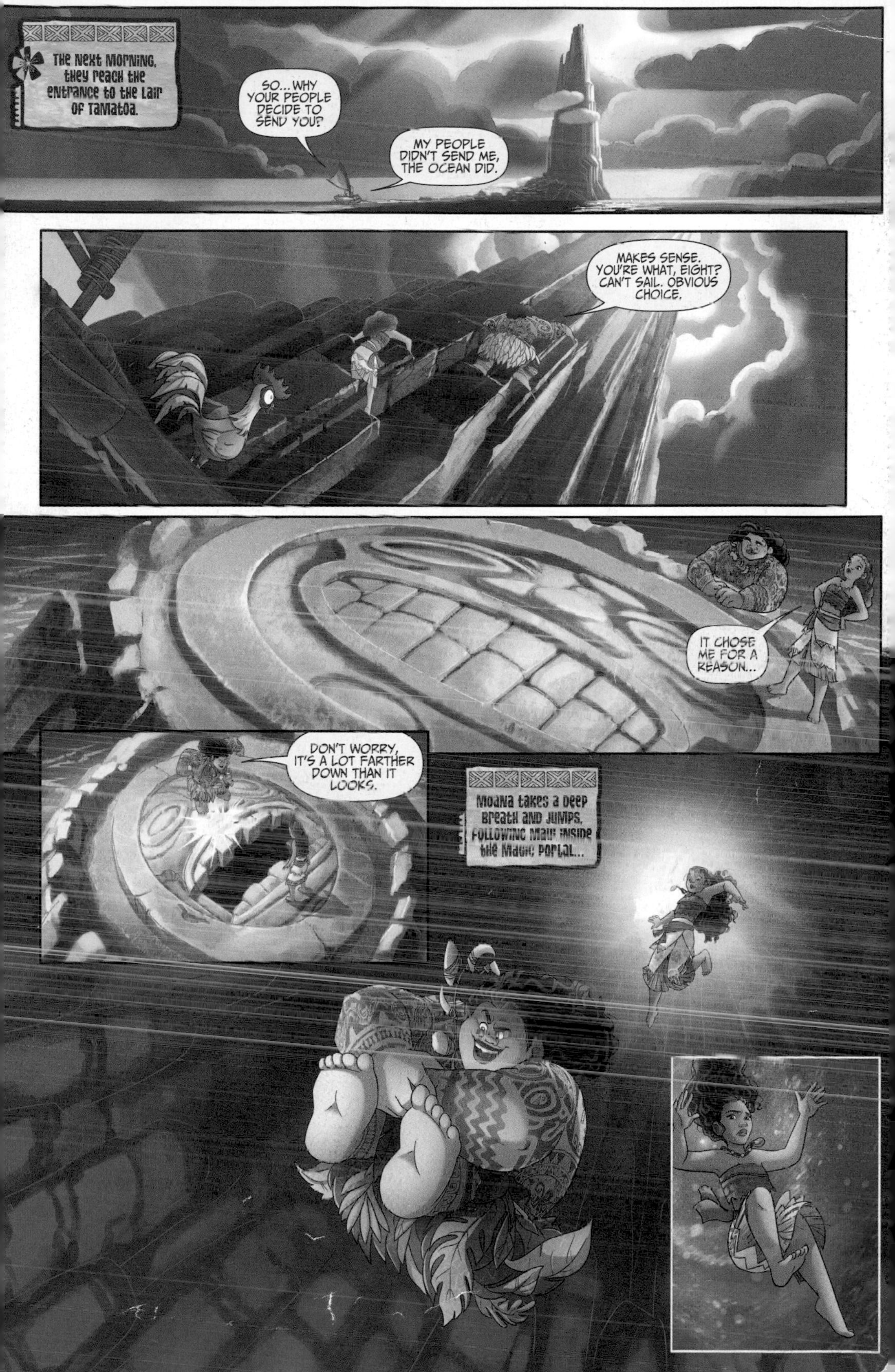
The Next Morning, they reach the entrance to the Lair of Tamatoa.
SO... WHY YOUR PEOPLE DECIDE TO SEND YOU?
MY PEOPLE DIDN'T SEND ME, THE OCEAN DID.
MAKES SENSE. YOU'RE WHAT, EIGHT? CAN'T SAIL. OBVIOUS CHOICE.
IT CHOSE ME FOR A REASON...
DON'T WORRY, IT'S A LOT FARTHER DOWN THAN IT LOOKS.
Moana takes a deep breath and jumps, following Maui inside the Magic portal...

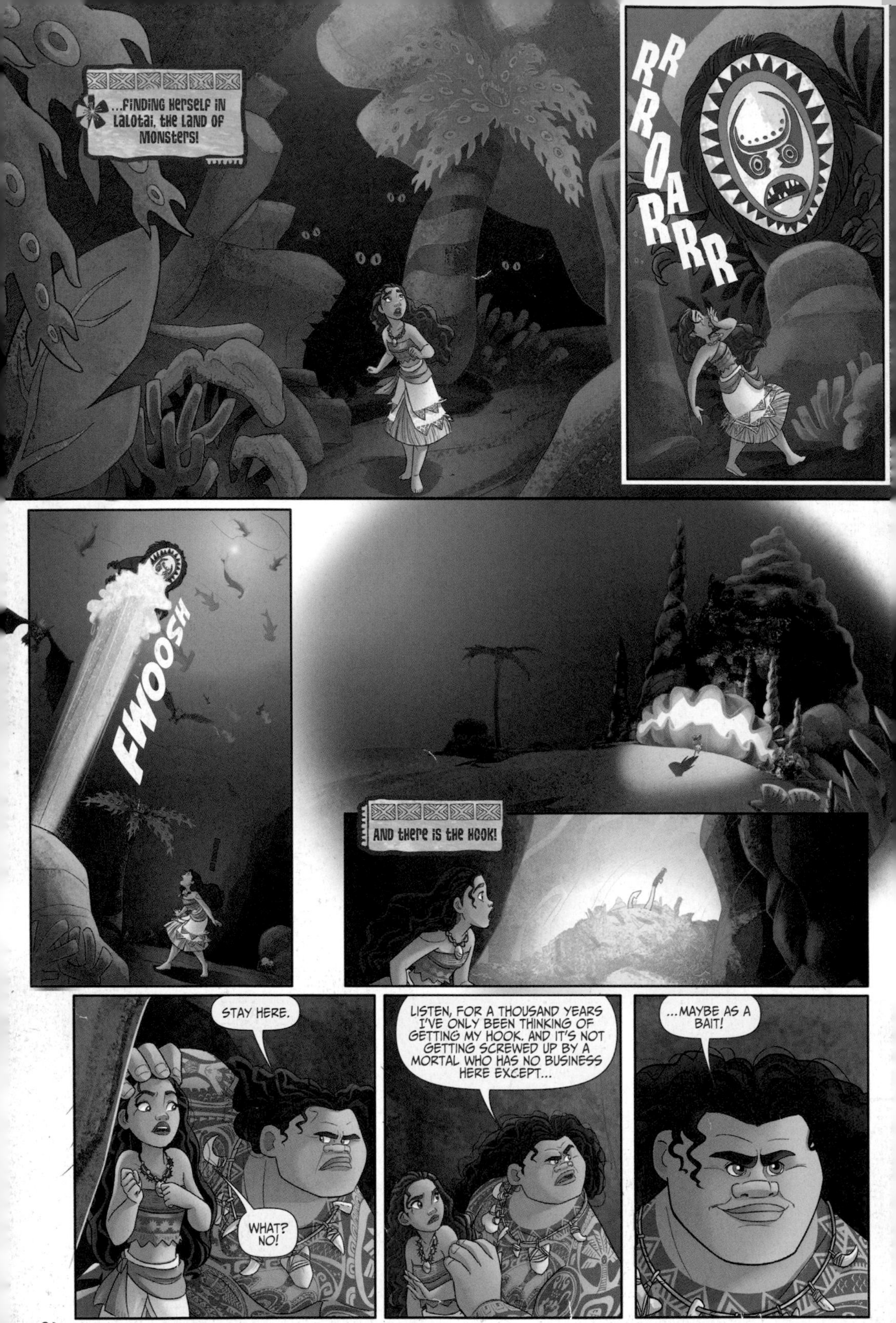

...FINDING HERSELF IN LALOTAI, THE LAND OF MONSTERS!
RRROARRR
FWOOSH
AND THERE IS THE HOOK!
STAY HERE.
WHAT? NO!
LISTEN, FOR A THOUSAND YEARS I'VE ONLY BEEN THINKING OF GETTING MY HOOK. AND IT'S NOT GETTING SCREWED UP BY A MORTAL WHO HAS NO BUSINESS HERE EXCEPT...
...MAYBE AS A BAIT!

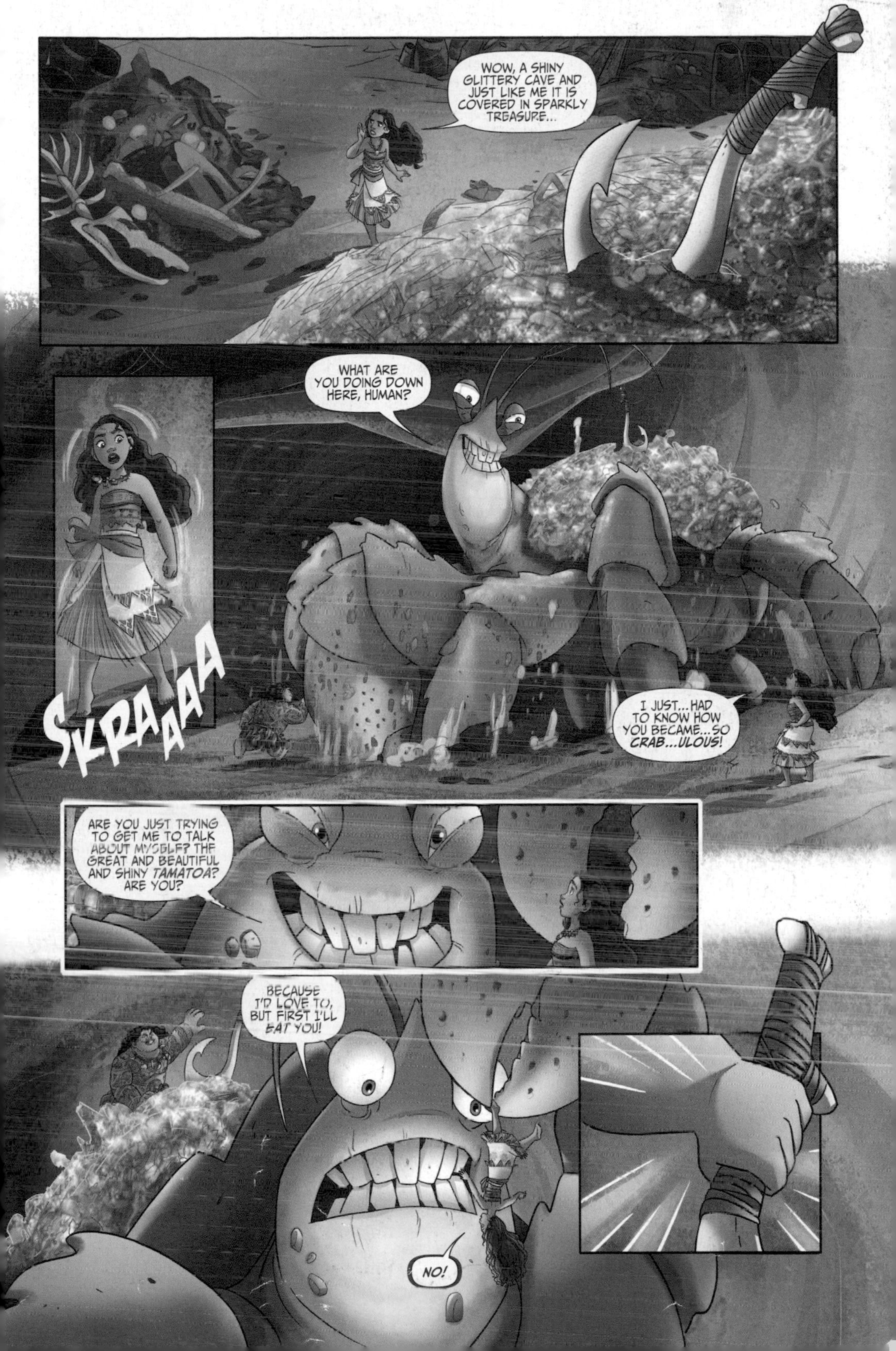
WOW, A SHINY GLITTERY CAVE AND JUST LIKE ME IT IS COVERED IN SPARKLY TREASURE...
WHAT ARE YOU DOING DOWN HERE, HUMAN?
SKRAAAA
I JUST...HAD TO KNOW HOW YOU BECAME...SO CRAB...ULOUS!
ARE YOU JUST TRYING TO GET ME TO TALK ABOUT MYSELF? THE GREAT AND BEAUTIFUL AND SHINY TAMATOA? ARE YOU?
BECAUSE I'D LOVE TO, BUT FIRST I'LL EAT YOU!
NO!

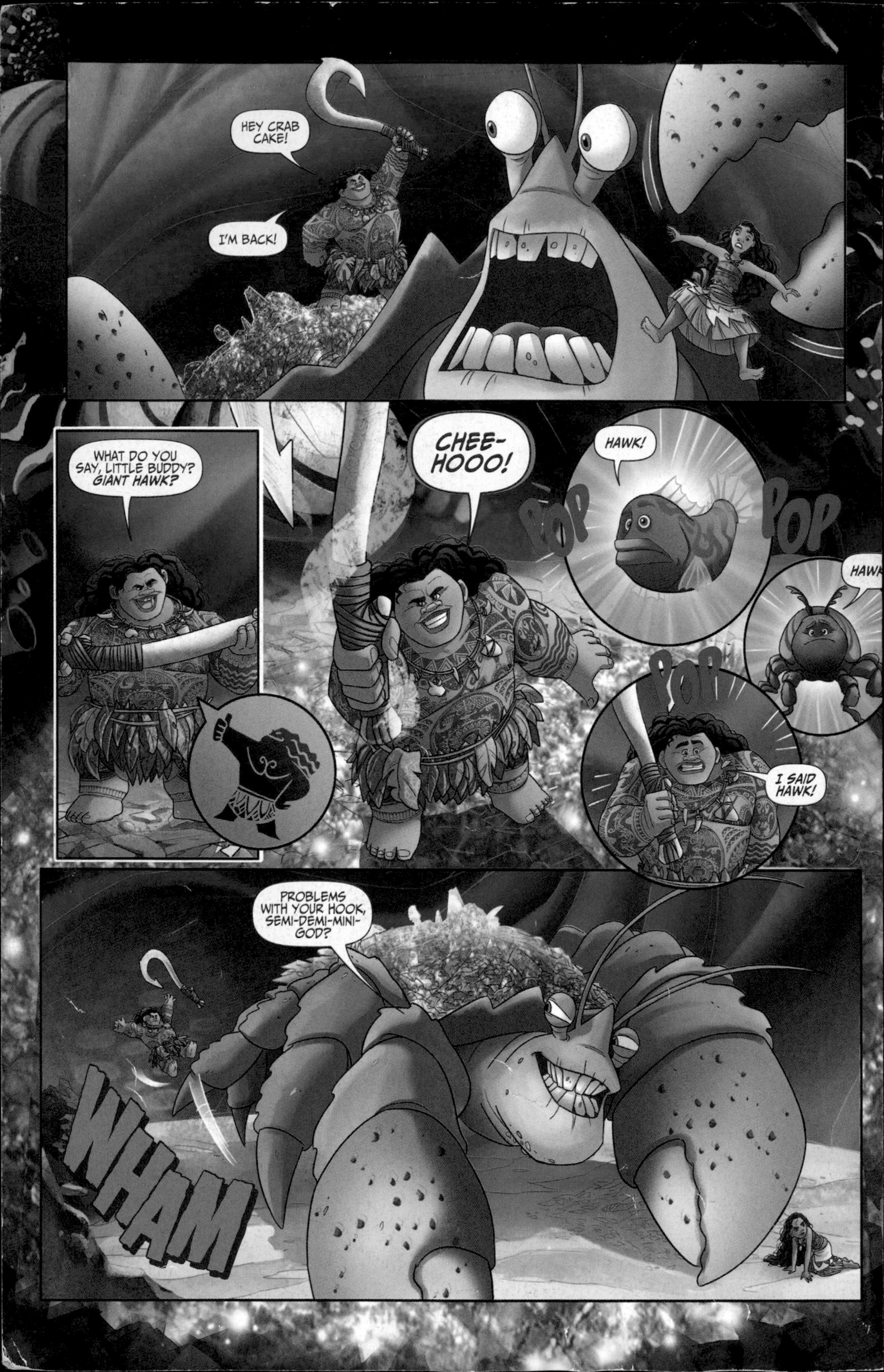
HEY CRAB CAKE!
I'M BACK!
WHAT DO YOU SAY, LITTLE BUDDY? GIANT HAWK?
CHEE-HOOO!
HAWK!
POP
POP
HAWK
POP
I SAID HAWK!
PROBLEMS WITH YOUR HOOK, SEMI-DEMI-MINI-GOD?
WHAM

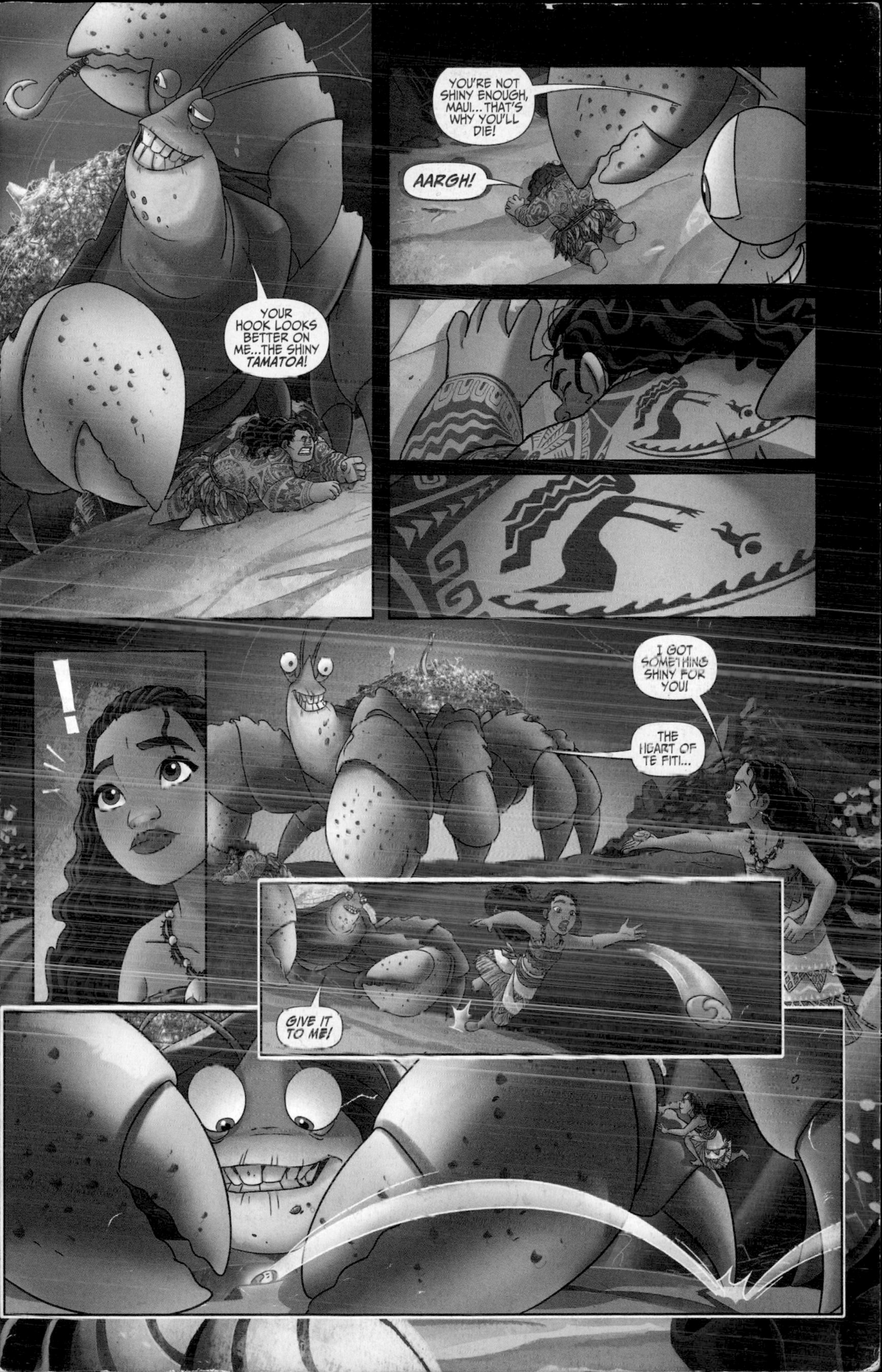
YOUR HOOK LOOKS BETTER ON ME...THE SHINY TAMATOA!
YOU'RE NOT SHINY ENOUGH, MAUI...THAT'S WHY YOU'LL DIE!
AARGH!
!
I GOT SOMETHING SHINY FOR YOU!
THE HEART OF TE FITI...
GIVE IT TO ME!

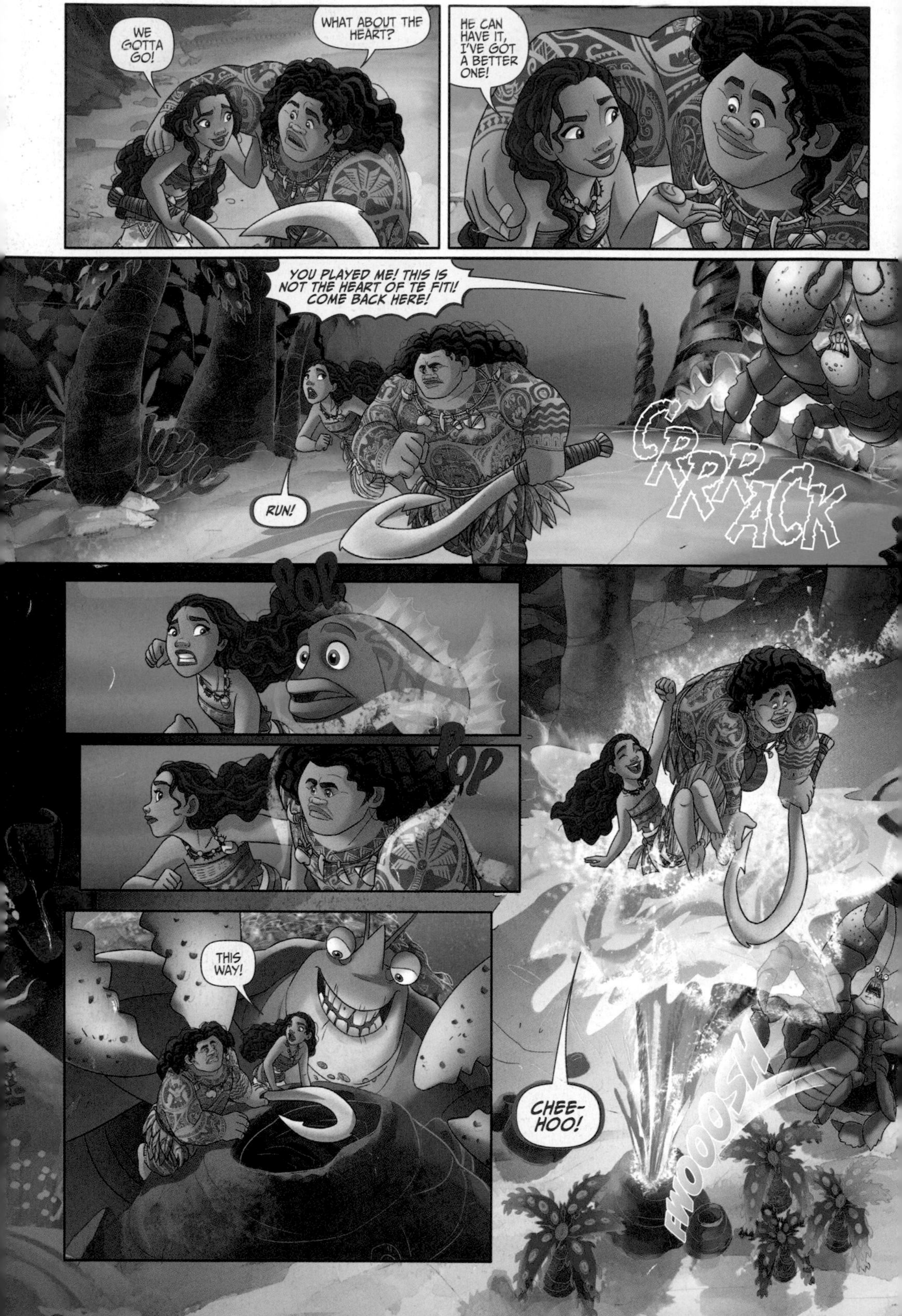
WE GOTTA GO!
WHAT ABOUT THE HEART?
HE CAN HAVE IT, I'VE GOT A BETTER ONE!
YOU PLAYED ME! THIS IS NOT THE HEART OF TE FITI! COME BACK HERE!
RUN!
CRRRACK
POP
POP
THIS WAY!
CHEE-HOO!
FWOOOSH

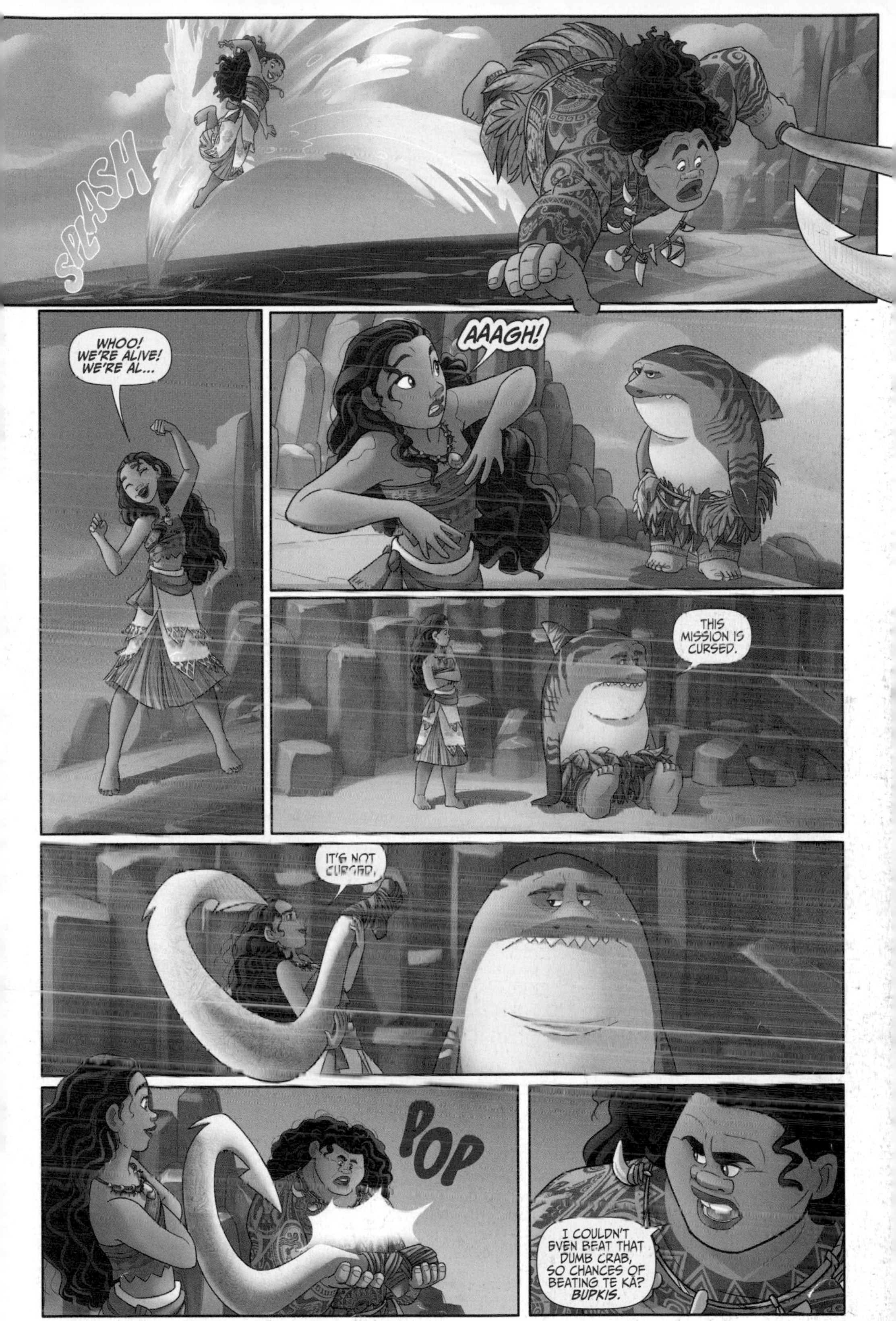
SPLASH
WHOO! WE'RE ALIVE! WE'RE AL...
AAAGH!
THIS MISSION IS CURSED.
IT'S NOT CURSED.
POP
I COULDN'T EVEN BEAT THAT DUMB CRAB, SO CHANCES OF BEATING TE KĀ? BUPKIS.

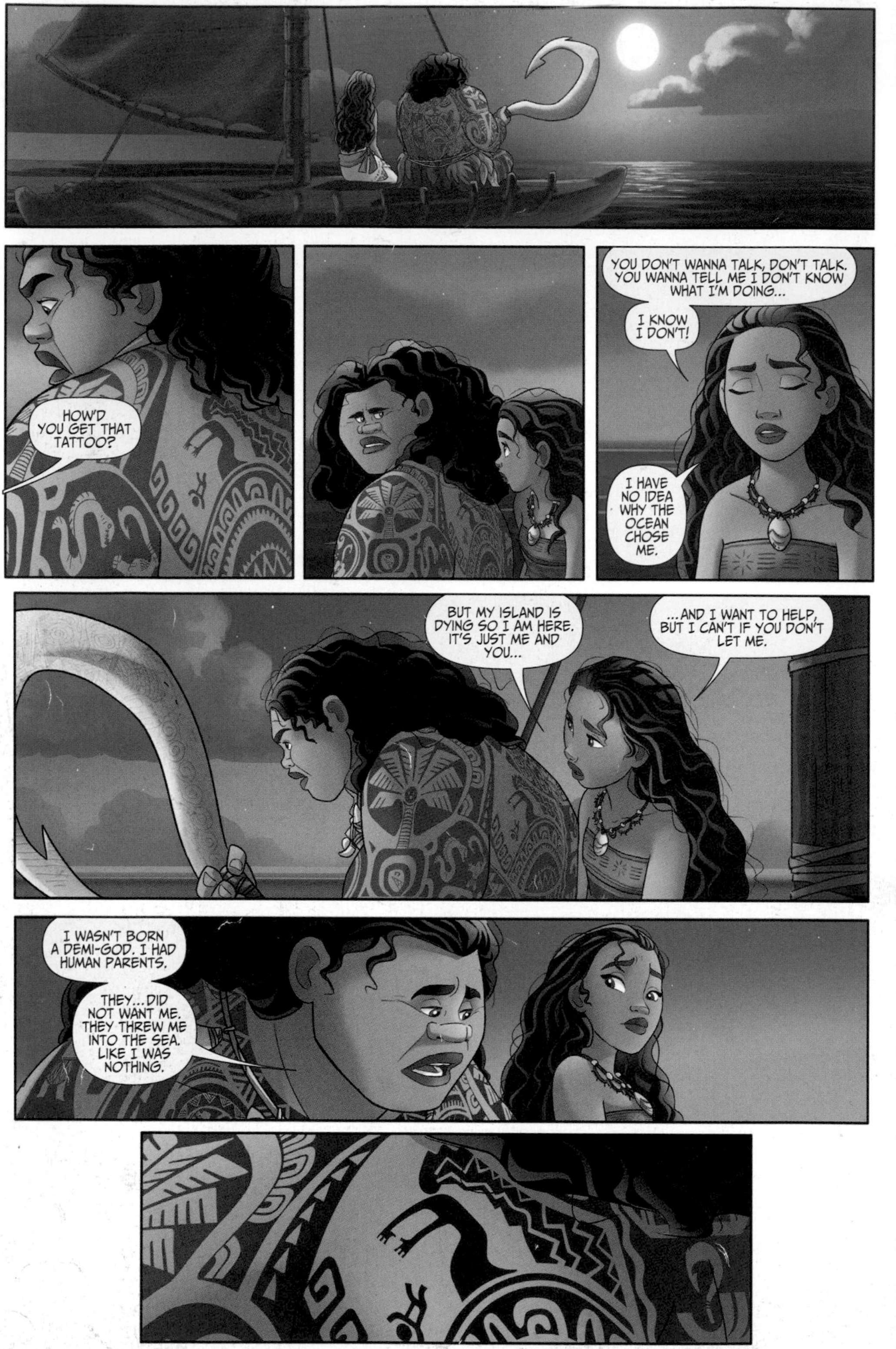
HOW'D YOU GET THAT TATTOO?
YOU DON'T WANNA TALK, DON'T TALK. YOU WANNA TELL ME I DON'T KNOW WHAT I'M DOING...
I KNOW I DON'T!
I HAVE NO IDEA WHY THE OCEAN CHOSE ME.
BUT MY ISLAND IS DYING SO I AM HERE. IT'S JUST ME AND YOU...
...AND I WANT TO HELP, BUT I CAN'T IF YOU DON'T LET ME.
I WASN'T BORN A DEMI-GOD. I HAD HUMAN PARENTS.
THEY...DID NOT WANT ME. THEY THREW ME INTO THE SEA. LIKE I WAS NOTHING.

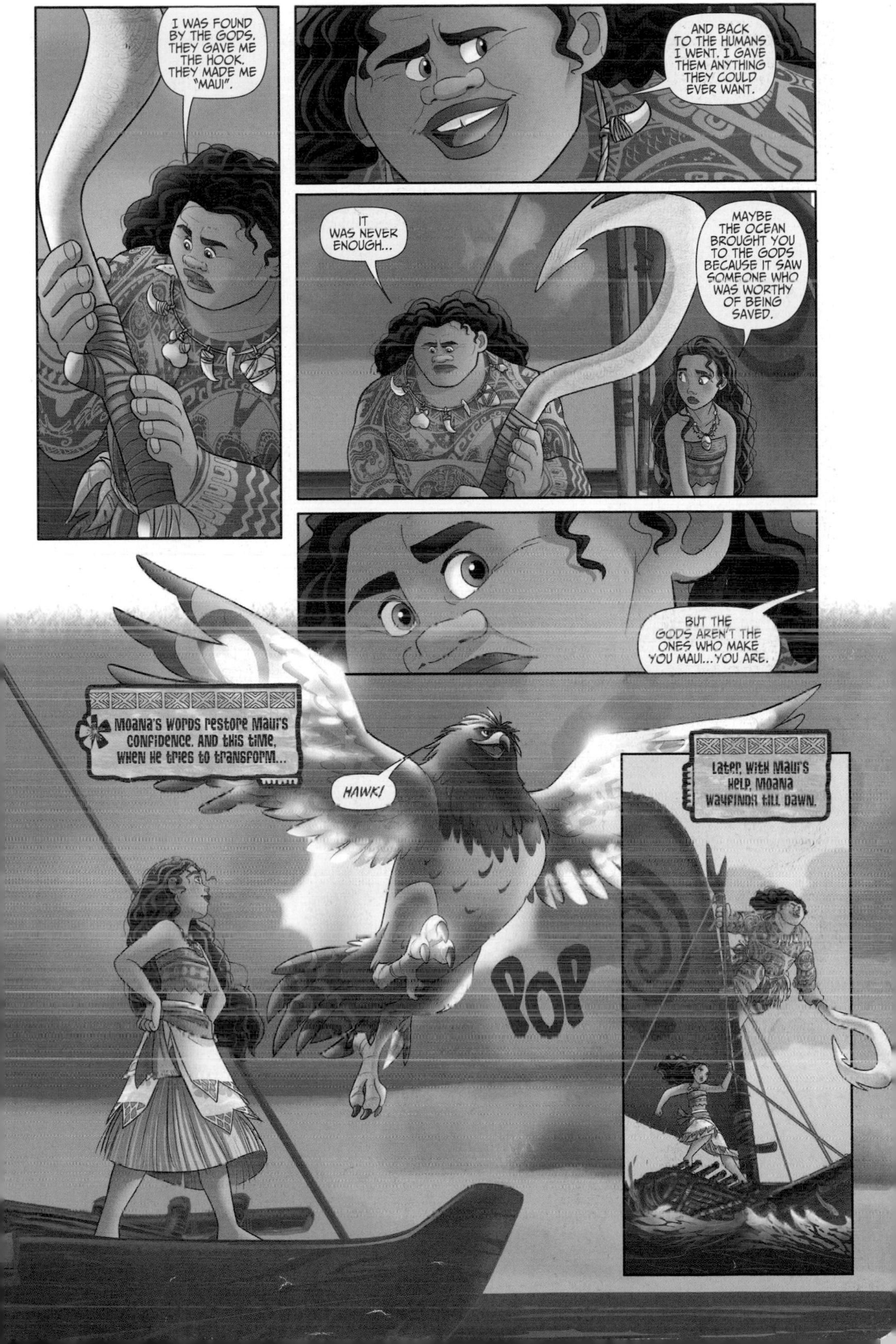
I WAS FOUND BY THE GODS. THEY GAVE ME THE HOOK. THEY MADE ME "MAUI".
AND BACK TO THE HUMANS I WENT. I GAVE THEM ANYTHING THEY COULD EVER WANT.
IT WAS NEVER ENOUGH...
MAYBE THE OCEAN BROUGHT YOU TO THE GODS BECAUSE IT SAW SOMEONE WHO WAS WORTHY OF BEING SAVED.
BUT THE GODS AREN'T THE ONES WHO MAKE YOU MAUI...YOU ARE.
Moana's words restore Maui's confidence. And this time, when he tries to transform...
HAWK!
POP
Later, with Maui's help, Moana wayfinds till dawn.

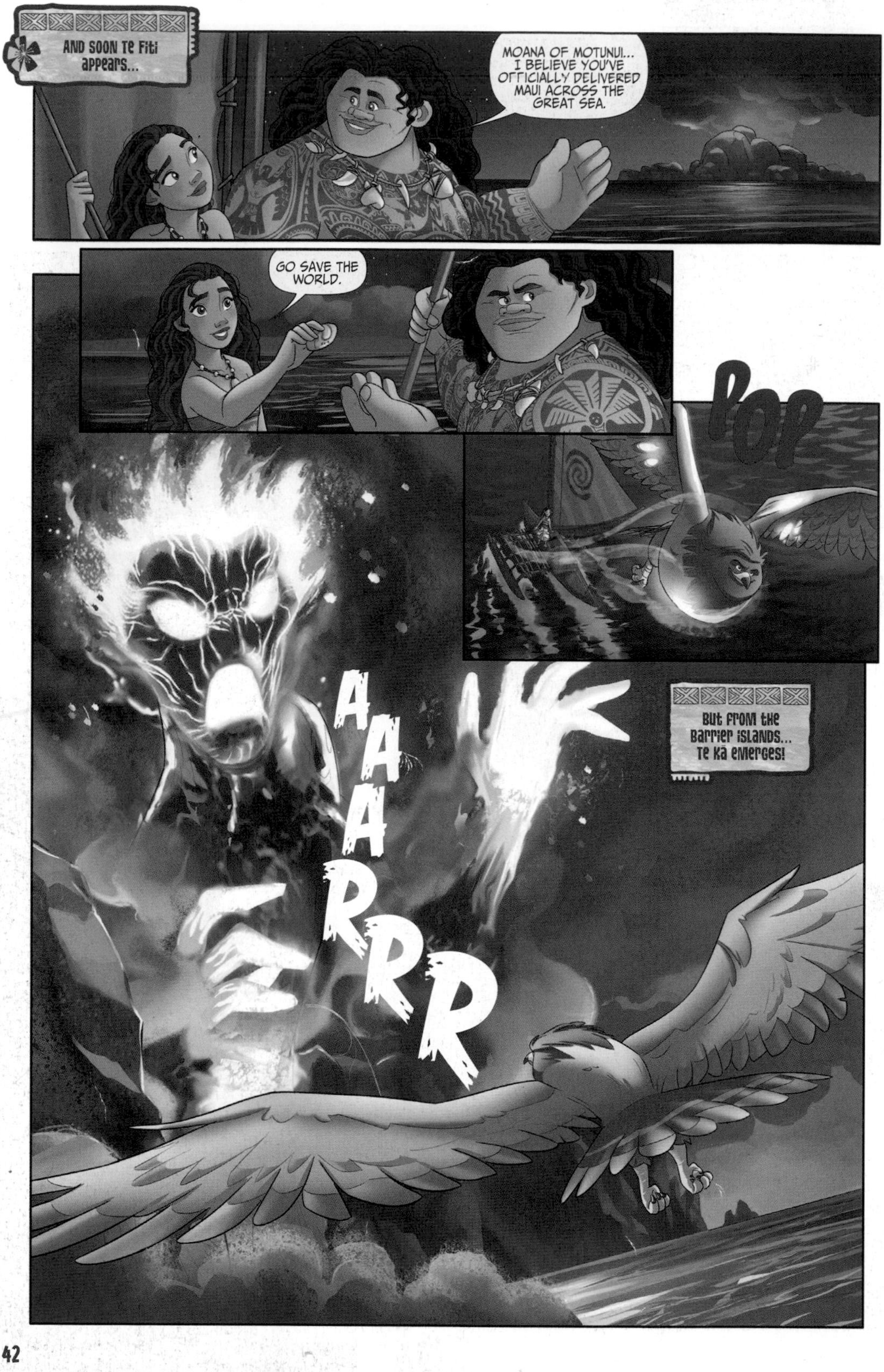
AND SOON TE FITI appears...
MOANA OF MOTUNUI... I BELIEVE YOU'VE OFFICIALLY DELIVERED MAUI ACROSS THE GREAT SEA.
GO SAVE THE WORLD.
POP
But from the Barrier islands... Te Kā emerges!
AAARRR

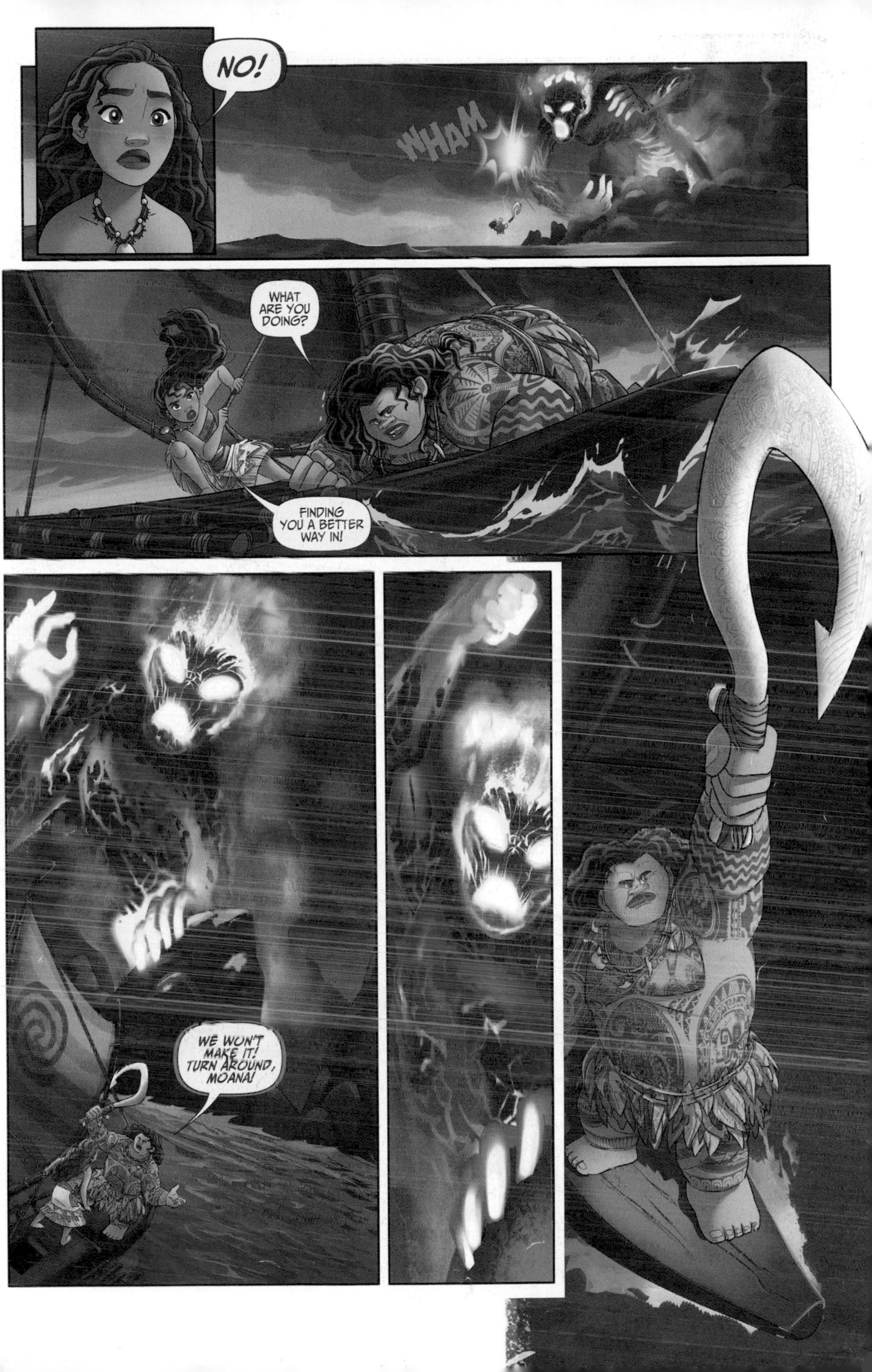
NO!
WHAM
WHAT ARE YOU DOING?
FINDING YOU A BETTER WAY IN!
WE WON'T MAKE IT! TURN AROUND, MOANA!

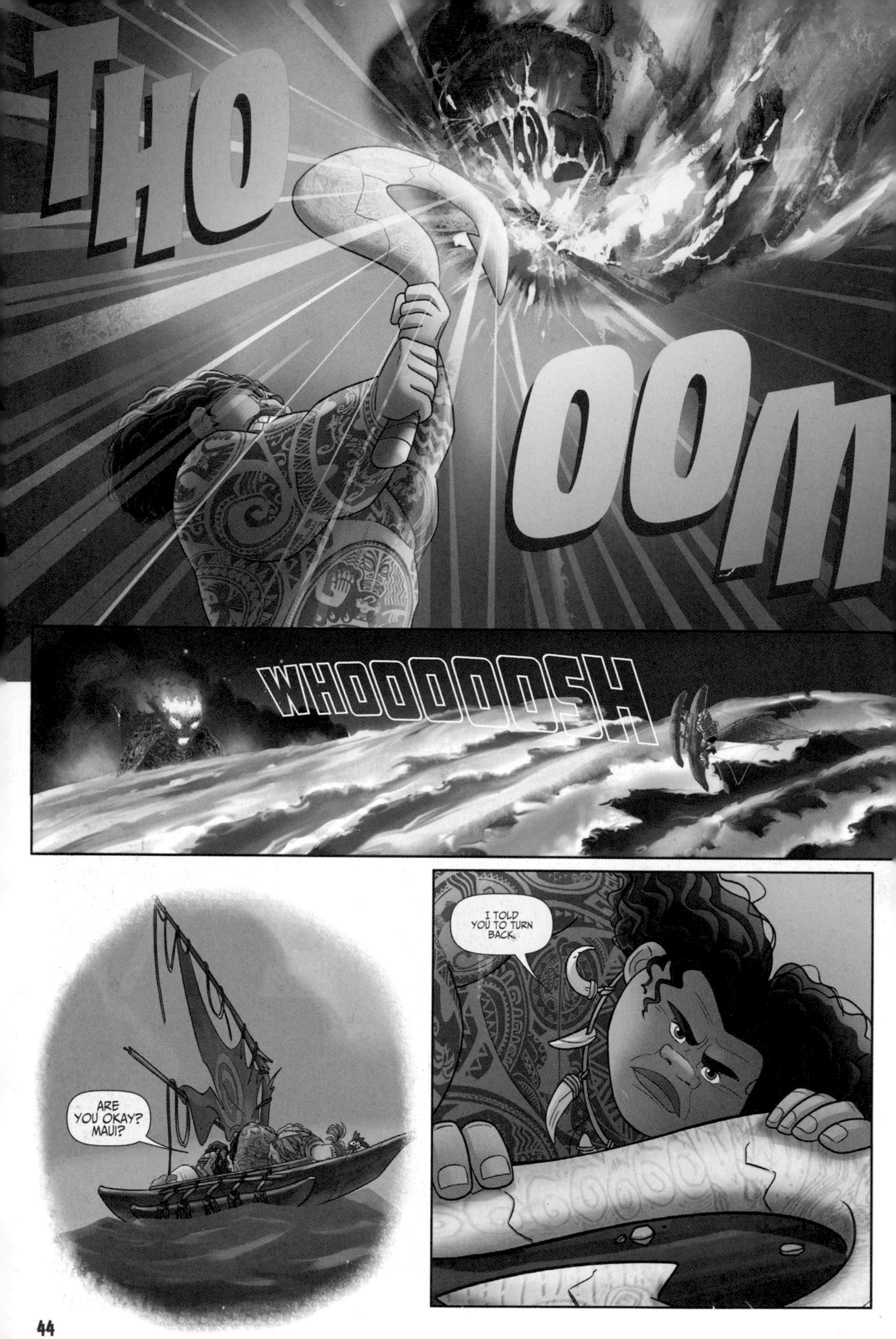
THO
OOM
WHOOOOOOSH
I TOLD YOU TO TURN BACK.
ARE YOU OKAY? MAUI?

NEXT TIME WE'LL BE MORE CAREFUL! TE KĀ IS LAVA, IT CAN'T GO IN THE WATER, WE CAN FIND A WAY AROUND...

I'M NOT GOING BACK! MY HOOK IS CRACKED, ONE MORE HIT AND IT'S OVER!

WITHOUT MY HOOK I'M NOTHING!

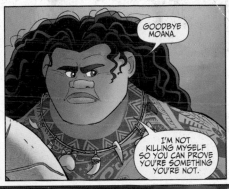

GOODBYE MOANA.

I'M NOT KILLING MYSELF SO YOU CAN PROVE YOU'RE SOMETHING YOU'RE NOT.

WHY DID YOU BRING ME HERE, OCEAN? I'M NOT THE RIGHT PERSON!

YOU HAVE TO CHOSE SOMEONE ELSE!

FSSHH

AS THE HEART OF TE FITI DISAPPEARS UNDERWATER MOANA REALIZES SHE FAILED EVERYONE.

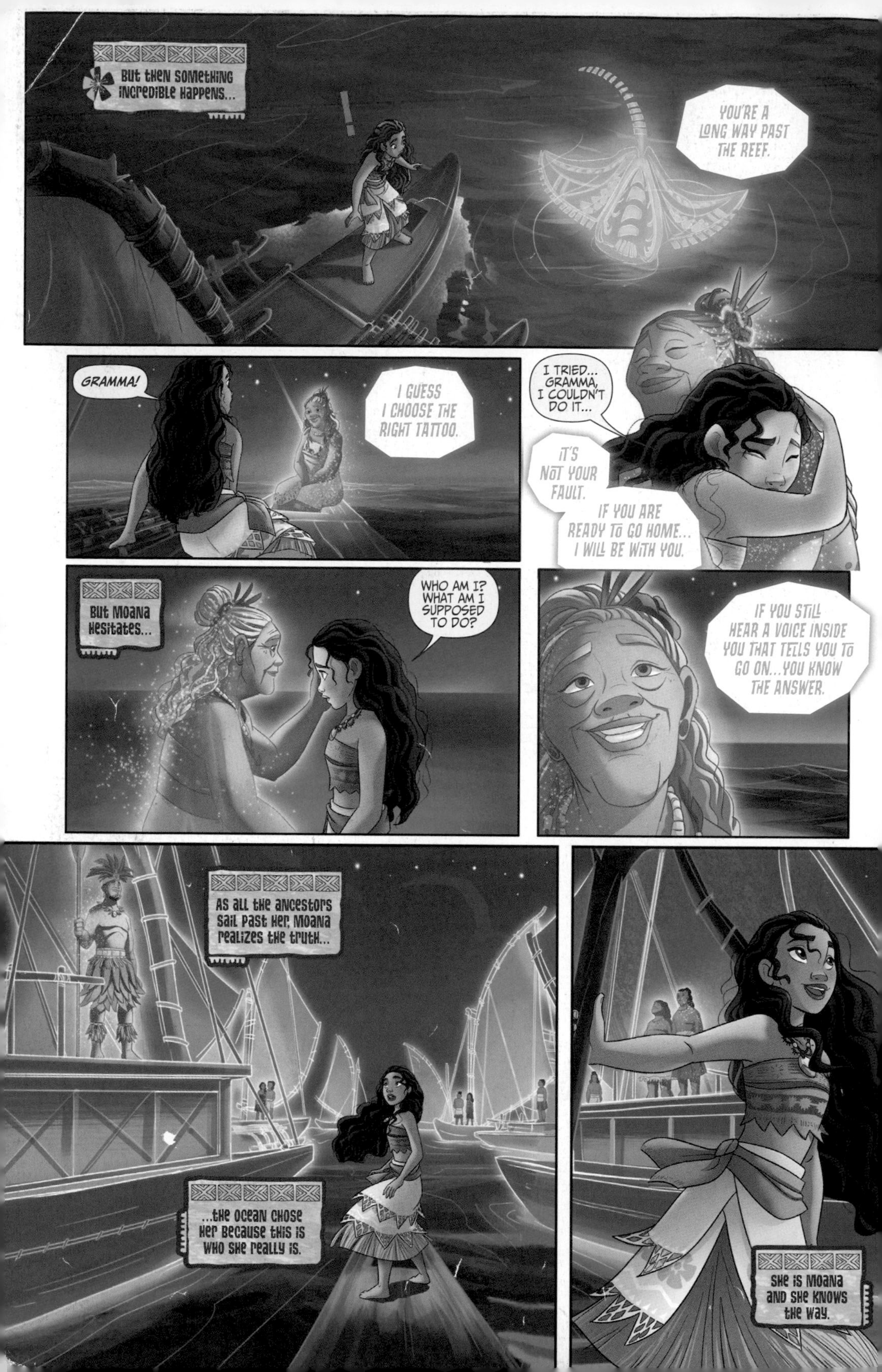
But then something incredible happens...
YOU'RE A LONG WAY PAST THE REEF.
GRAMMA!
I GUESS I CHOOSE THE RIGHT TATTOO.
I TRIED... GRAMMA, I COULDN'T DO IT...
IT'S NOT YOUR FAULT.
IF YOU ARE READY TO GO HOME... I WILL BE WITH YOU.
But Moana hesitates...
WHO AM I? WHAT AM I SUPPOSED TO DO?
IF YOU STILL HEAR A VOICE INSIDE YOU THAT TELLS YOU TO GO ON...YOU KNOW THE ANSWER.
As all the ancestors sail past her, Moana realizes the truth...
...the ocean chose her because this is who she really is.
She is Moana and she knows the way.

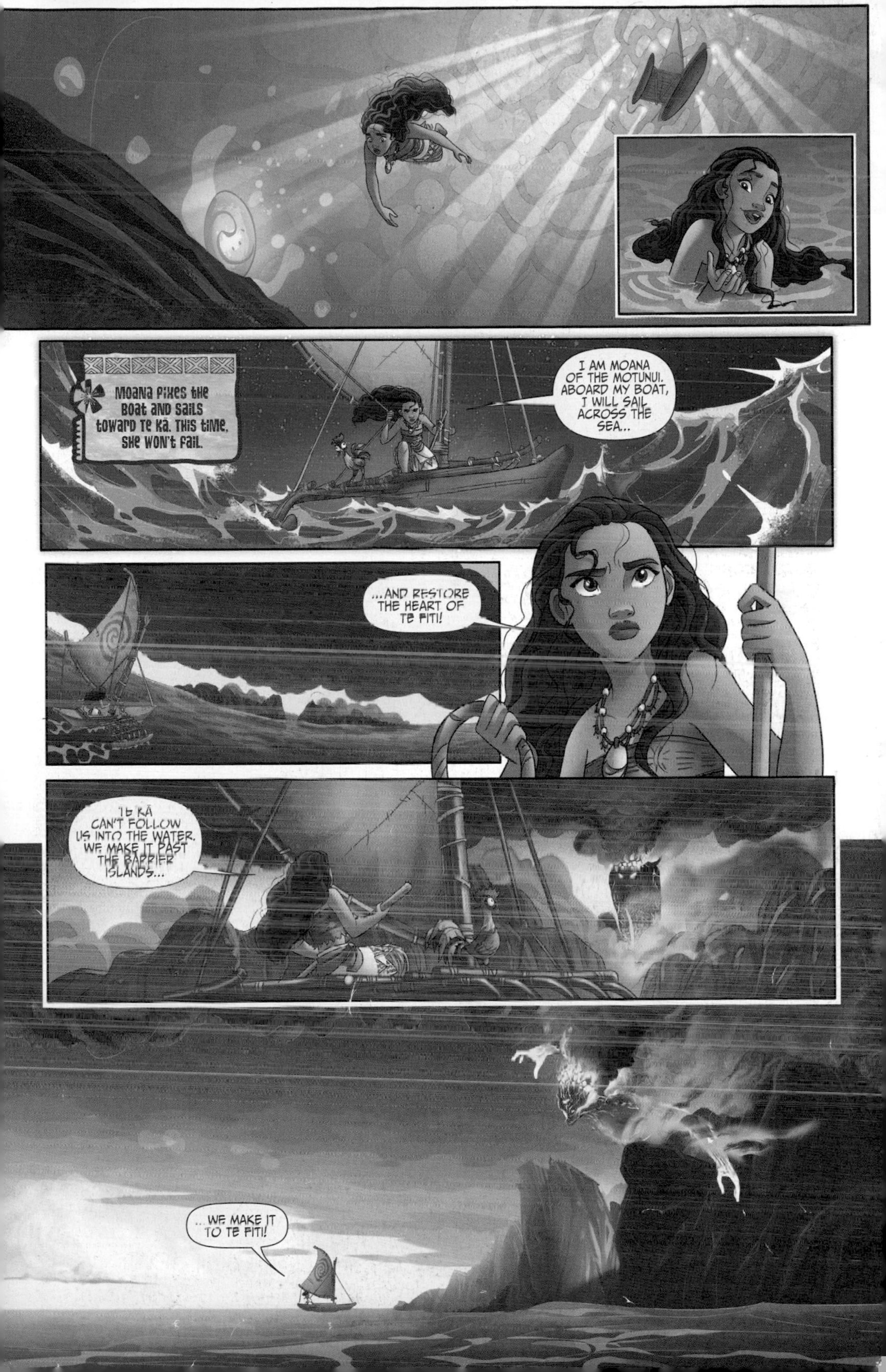

Moana fixes the boat and sails toward Te Kā. This time, she won't fail.
I AM MOANA OF THE MOTUNUI. ABOARD MY BOAT, I WILL SAIL ACROSS THE SEA...
...AND RESTORE THE HEART OF TE FITI!
TE KĀ CAN'T FOLLOW US INTO THE WATER. WE MAKE IT PAST THE BARRIER ISLANDS...
...WE MAKE IT TO TE FITI!

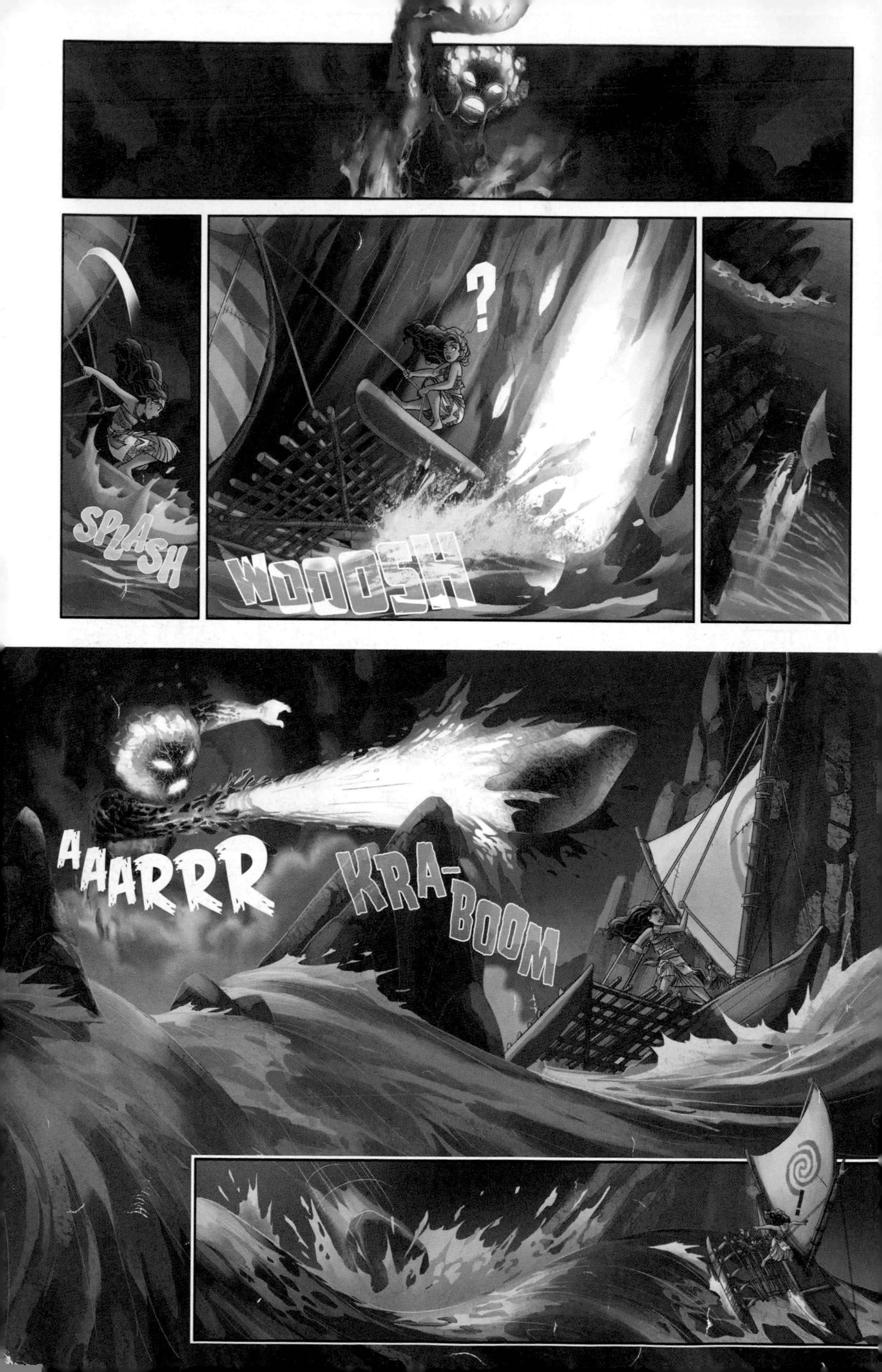
SPLASH
?
WOOOSH
AAARRR
KRA-BOOM
!

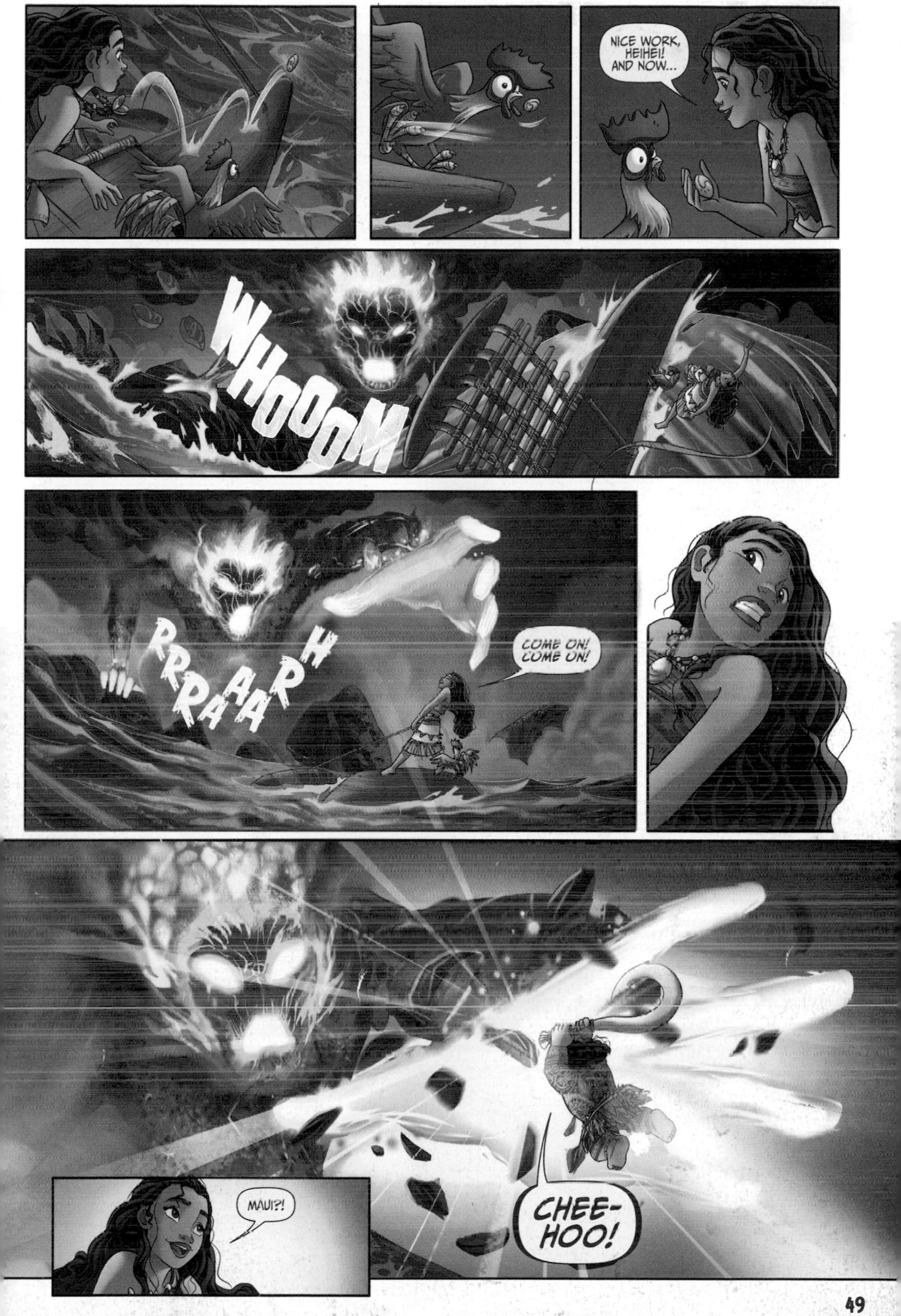
NICE WORK, HEIHEI! AND NOW...
WHOOOM
RRRAAARH
COME ON! COME ON!
MAUI?!
CHEE-HOO!

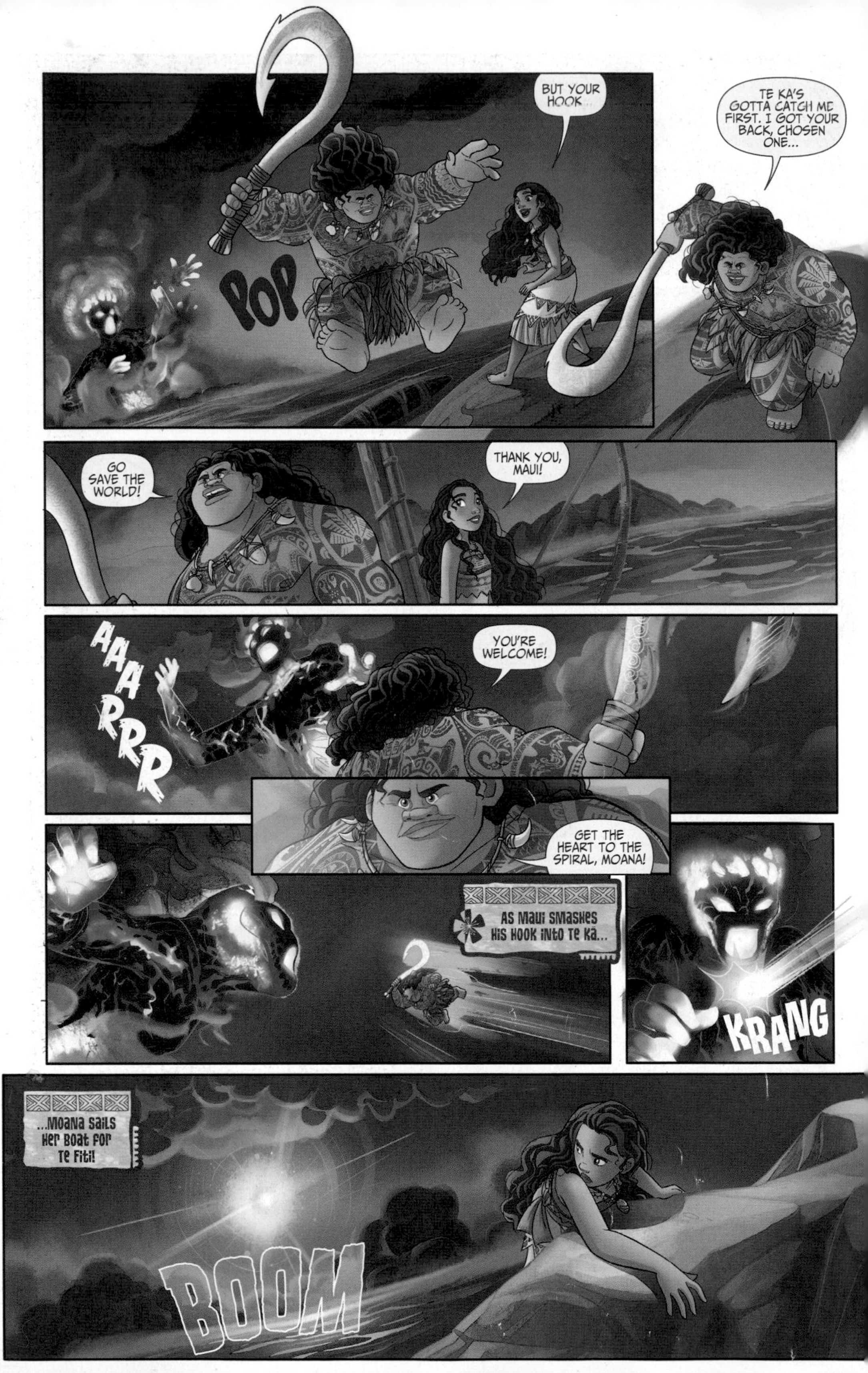
BUT YOUR HOOK...
TE KA'S GOTTA CATCH ME FIRST. I GOT YOUR BACK, CHOSEN ONE...
POP
GO SAVE THE WORLD!
THANK YOU, MAUI!
AAAARRR
YOU'RE WELCOME!
GET THE HEART TO THE SPIRAL, MOANA!
AS MAUI SMASHES HIS HOOK INTO TE KĀ...
KRANG
...MOANA SAILS HER BOAT FOR TE FITI!
BOOM

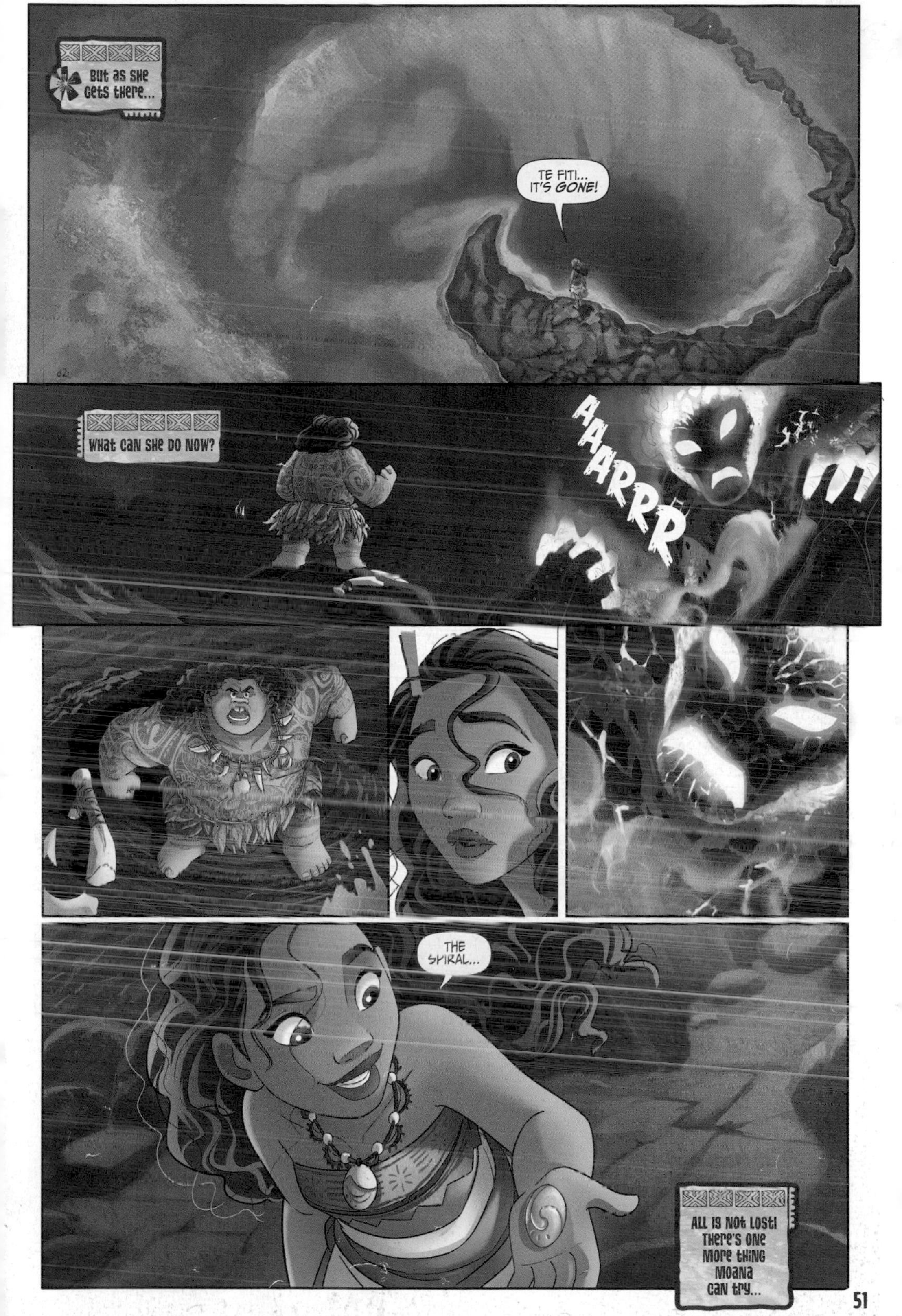
But as she gets there...
TE FITI... IT'S GONE!
What can she do now?
AAARRR
THE SPIRAL...
All is not lost! There's one more thing Moana can try...

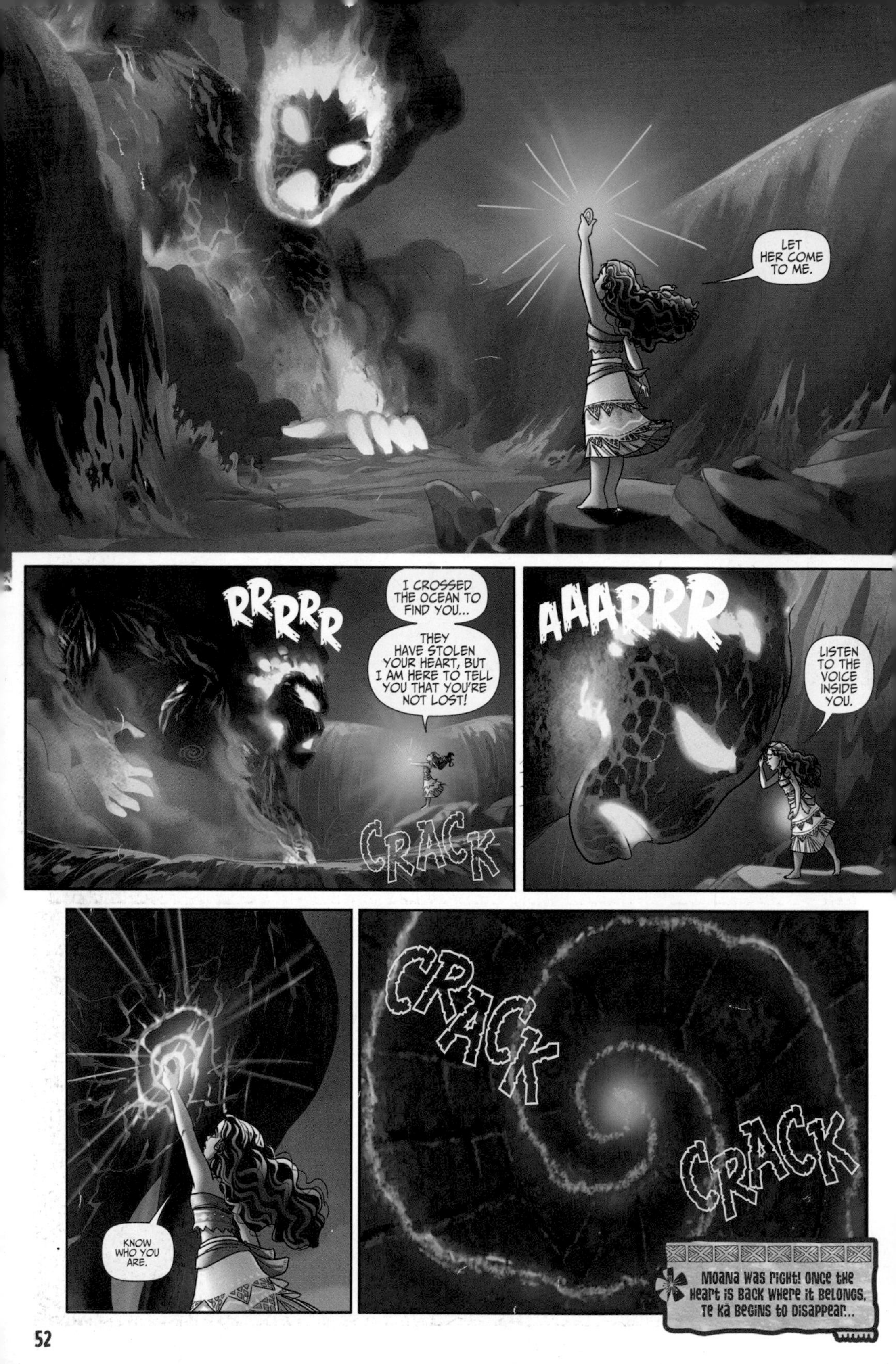

LET HER COME TO ME.
RRRRR
I CROSSED THE OCEAN TO FIND YOU...
THEY HAVE STOLEN YOUR HEART, BUT I AM HERE TO TELL YOU THAT YOU'RE NOT LOST!
CRACK
AAARRR
LISTEN TO THE VOICE INSIDE YOU.
KNOW WHO YOU ARE.
CRACK
CRACK
Moana was right! Once the heart is back where it belongs, Te Ka begins to disappear...

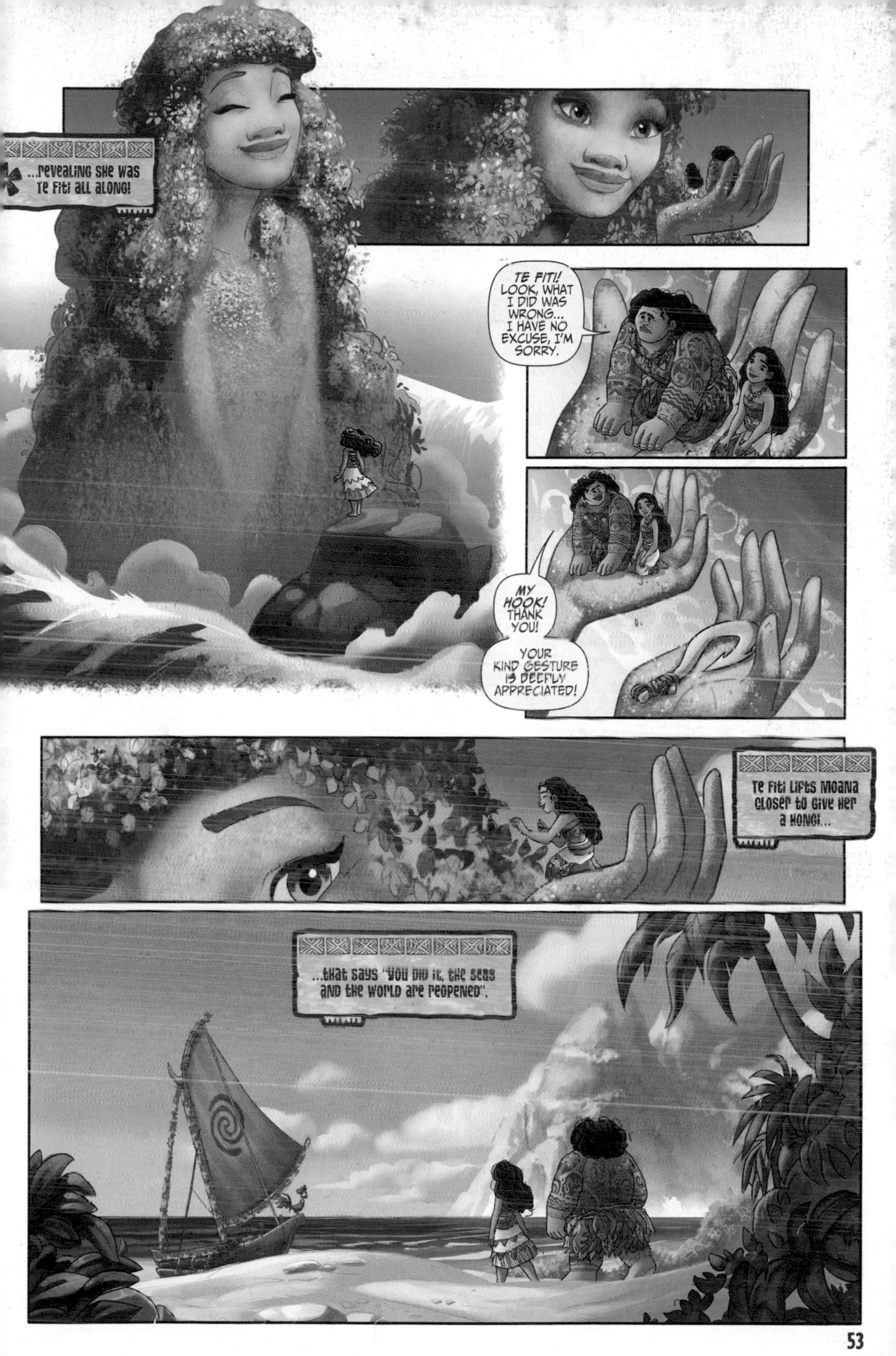

...revealing she was Te Fiti all along!
TE FITI! LOOK, WHAT I DID WAS WRONG... I HAVE NO EXCUSE, I'M SORRY.
MY HOOK! THANK YOU!
YOUR KIND GESTURE IS DEEPLY APPRECIATED!
Te Fiti lifts Moana closer to give her a hongi...
...that says "you did it, the seas and the world are reopened".

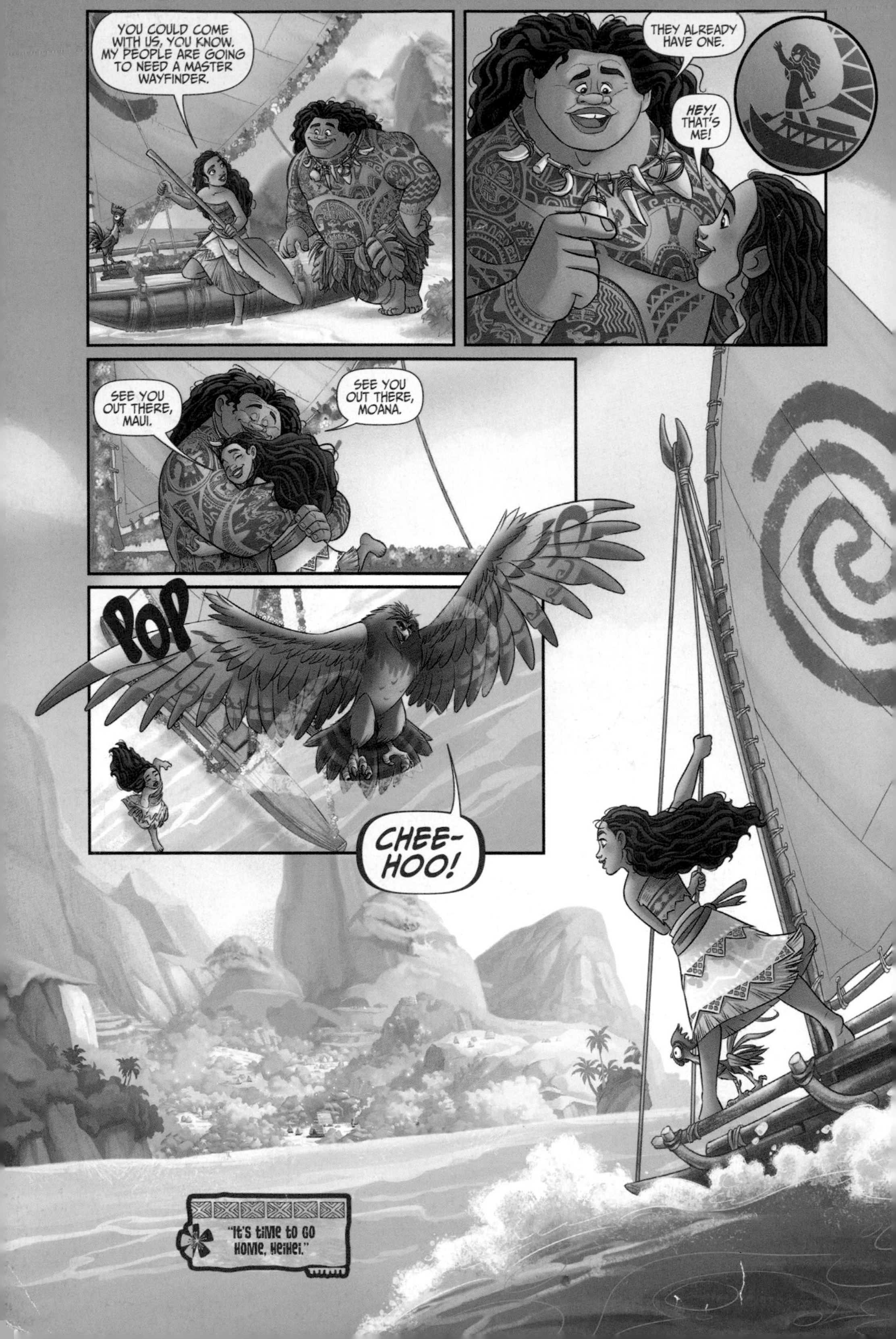
YOU COULD COME WITH US, YOU KNOW. MY PEOPLE ARE GOING TO NEED A MASTER WAYFINDER.
THEY ALREADY HAVE ONE.
HEY! THAT'S ME!
SEE YOU OUT THERE, MAUI.
SEE YOU OUT THERE, MOANA.
POP
CHEE-HOO!
"It's time to go home, Heihei."

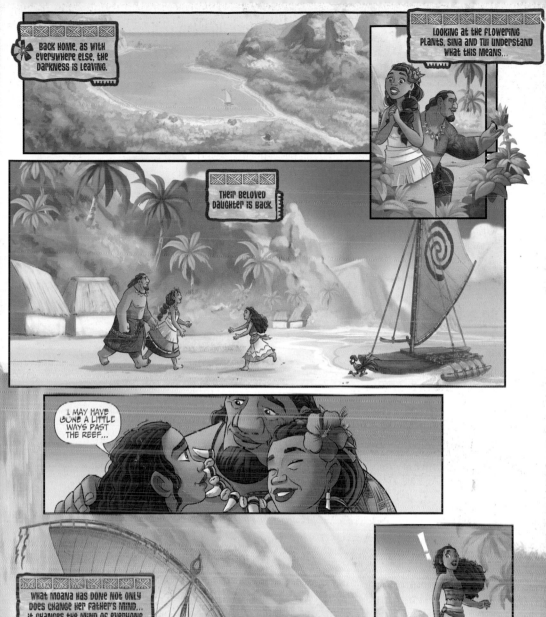

BACK HOME, AS WITH EVERYWHERE ELSE, THE DARKNESS IS LEAVING.

LOOKING AT THE FLOWERING PLANTS, SINA AND TUI UNDERSTAND WHAT THIS MEANS...

THEIR BELOVED DAUGHTER IS BACK.

I MAY HAVE GONE A LITTLE WAYS PAST THE REEF...

WHAT MOANA HAS DONE NOT ONLY DOES CHANGE HER FATHER'S MIND... IT CHANGES THE MIND OF EVERYONE.

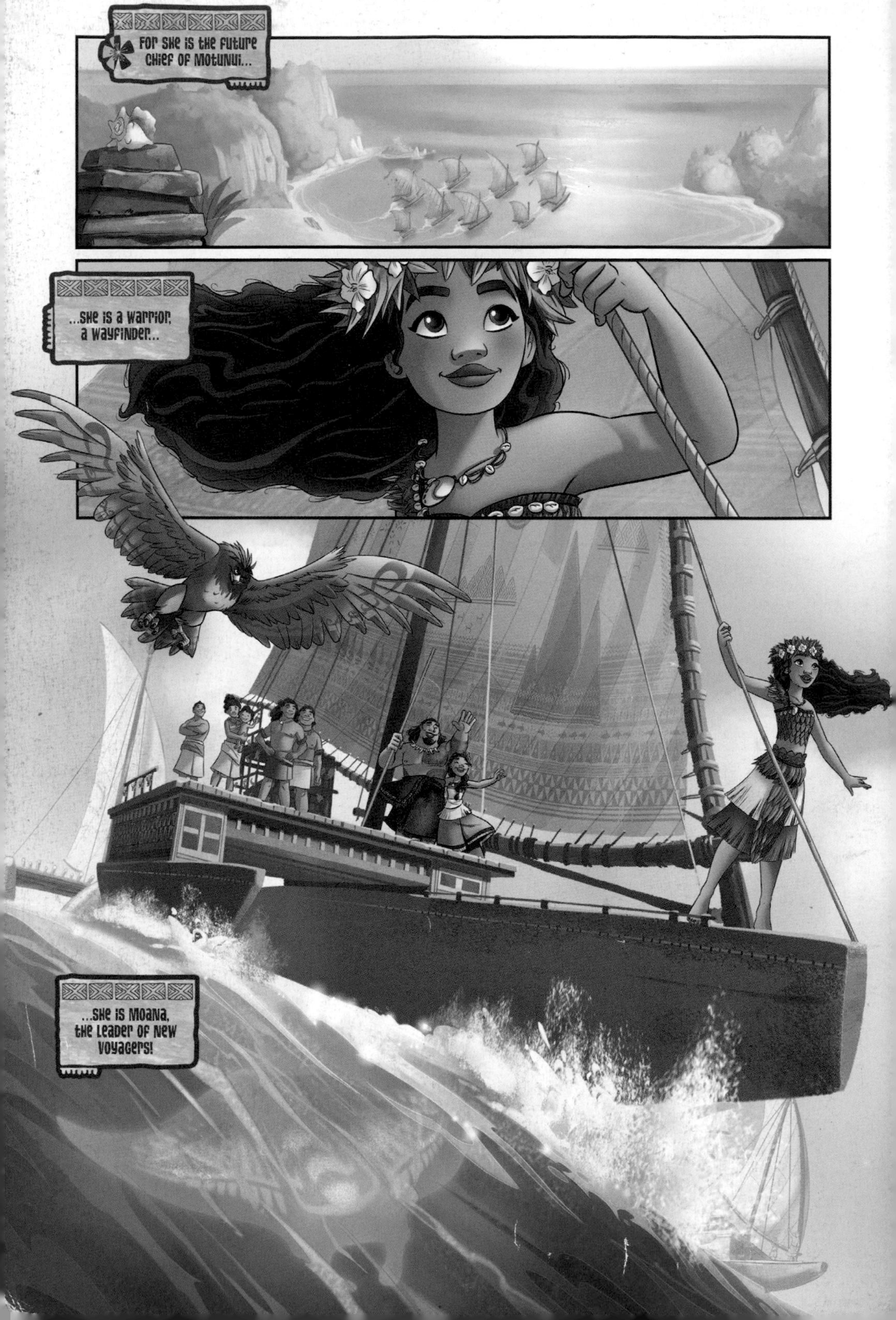
For she is the future chief of Motunui...
...she is a warrior, a wayfinder...
...she is Moana, the leader of new voyagers!

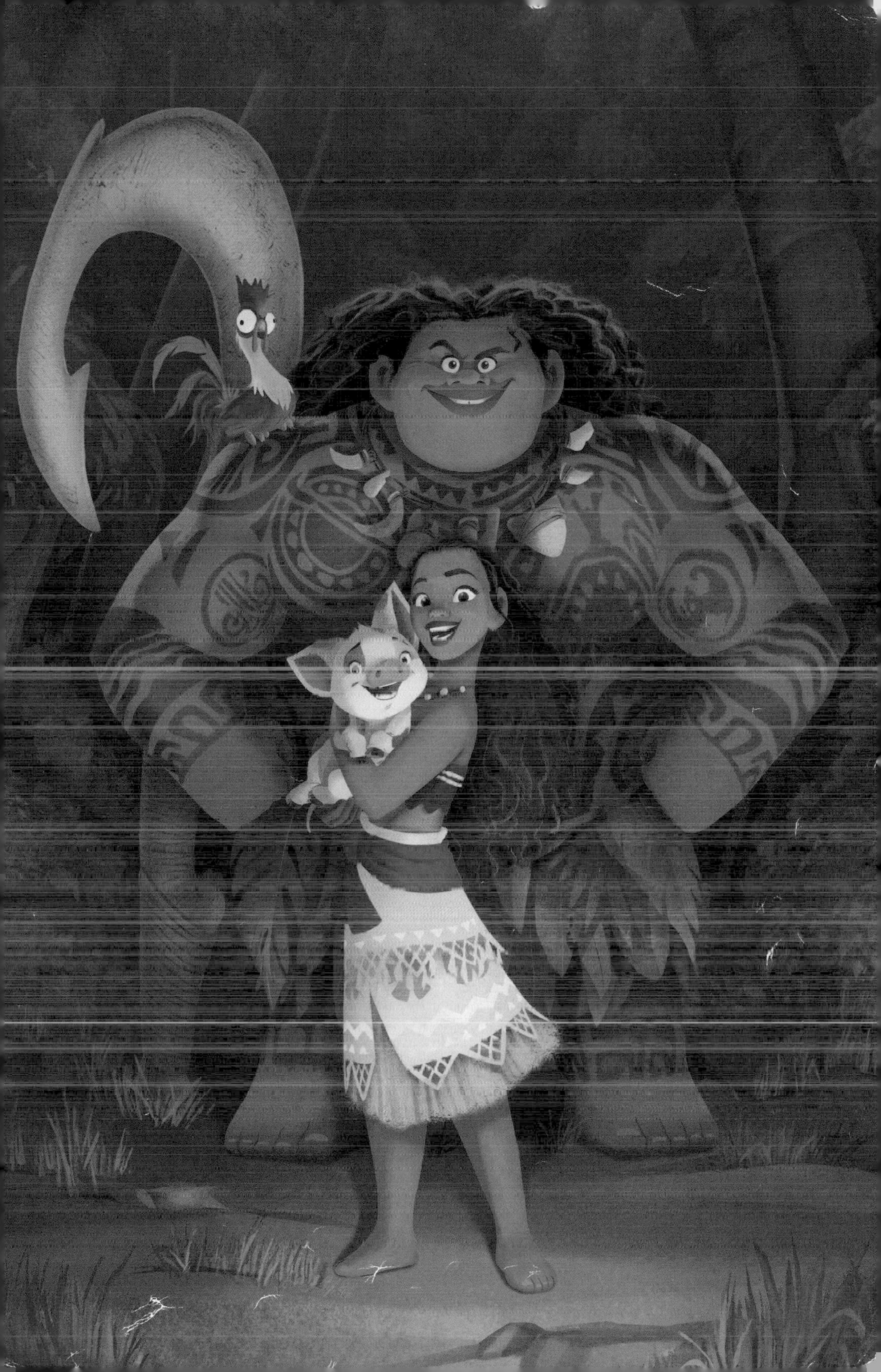

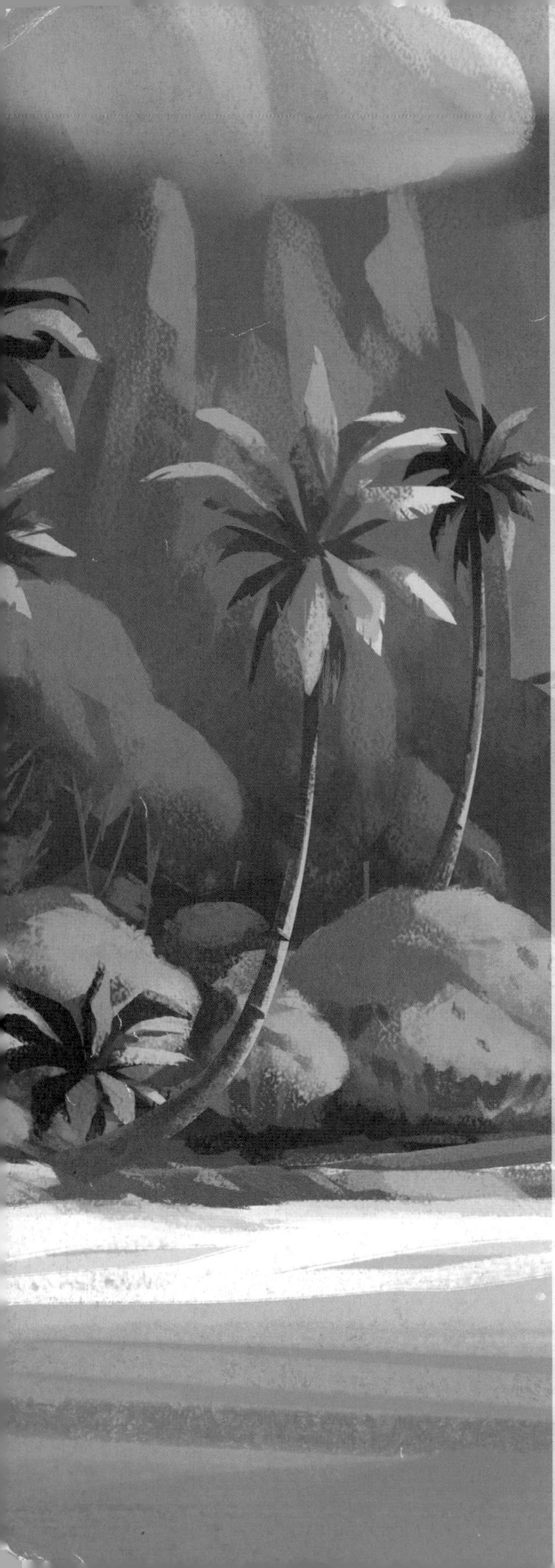

THE GRAPHIC NOVEL

MANUSCRIPT ADAPTATION:
Alessandro Ferrari

LAYOUT
Alberto Zanon, Giada Perissinotto

PENCIL/INKING
Veronica Di Lorenzo, Luca Bertelè

COLOR
BACKGROUNDS: Massimo Rocca, PierLuigi Casolino, Pasquale Desiato, Maria Claudia Di Genova

CHARACTERS: Dario Calabria

COVER LAYOUT
Alberto Zanon

PENCIL/INKING
Luca Bertelè

COLOR
Grzegorz Krysinsky

GRAFICH DESIGN & EDITORIAL
Red·Spot Srl - Milan, Italy, Chris Dickey (Lettering)

PRE-PRESS
Red·Spot Srl - Milan, Italy, Litomilano S.r.l.

SPECIAL THANKS TO
Osnat Shurer, Andy Harkness, Ian Gooding, Bill Schwab, Mayka Mei, Blair Bradley, Ryan Gilleland, Alison Giordano, Monica Vasquez

DISNEY PUBLISHING WORLDWIDE
Global Magazines, Comics and Partworks

PUBLISHER
Gianfranco Cordara

EXECUTIVE EDITOR
Carlotta Quattrocolo

EDITORIAL TEAM
Bianca Coletti (Director, Magazines), Guido Frazzini (Director, Comics), Stefano Ambrosio (Executive Editor, New IP), Camilla Vedove (Senior Manager, Editorial Development), Behnoosh Khalili (Senior Editor), Julie Dorris (Senior Editor)

DESIGN
Enrico Soave (Senior Designer)
Manny Mederos (Creative Manager)

ART
Ken Shue (VP, Global Art), Roberto Santillo (Creative Director), Marco Ghiglione (Creative Manager), Stefano Attardi (Illustration manager)

PORTFOLIO MANAGEMENT
Olivia Ciancarelli (Director)

BUSINESS & MARKETING
Mariantonietta Galla (Marketing Manager), Virpi Korhonen (Editorial Manager), Kristen Ginter (Operations Manager)

CONTRIBUTORS
Simona Grandi, Amy Kim, Valeria Perrone

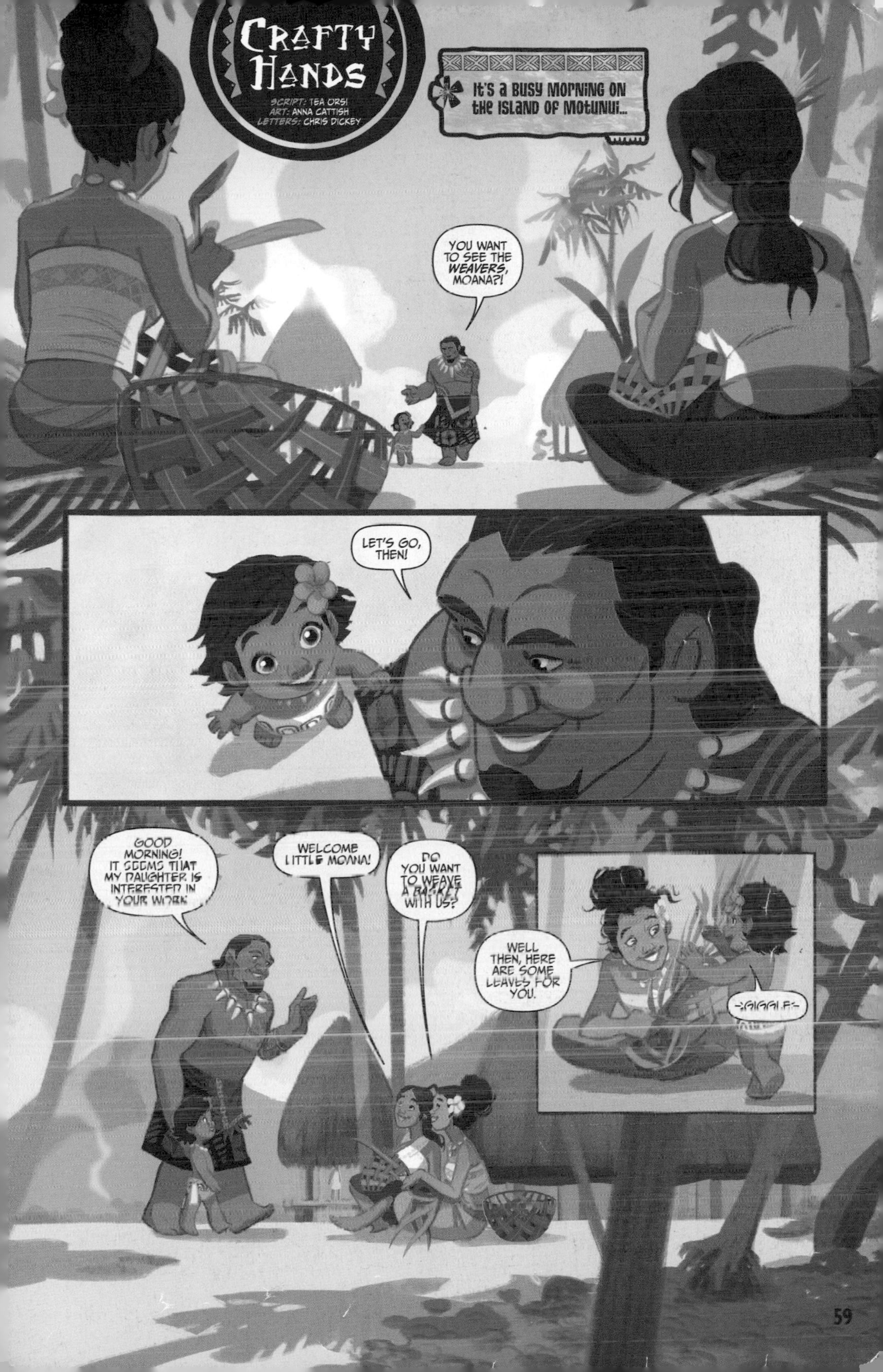
CRAFTY HANDS
SCRIPT: TEA ORSI
ART: ANNA CATTISH
LETTERS: CHRIS DICKEY
IT'S A BUSY MORNING ON THE ISLAND OF MOTUNUI...
YOU WANT TO SEE THE WEAVERS, MOANA?!
LET'S GO, THEN!
GOOD MORNING! IT SEEMS THAT MY DAUGHTER IS INTERESTED IN YOUR WORK
WELCOME LITTLE MOANA!
DO YOU WANT TO WEAVE A BASKET WITH US?
WELL THEN, HERE ARE SOME LEAVES FOR YOU.
-GIGGLE-

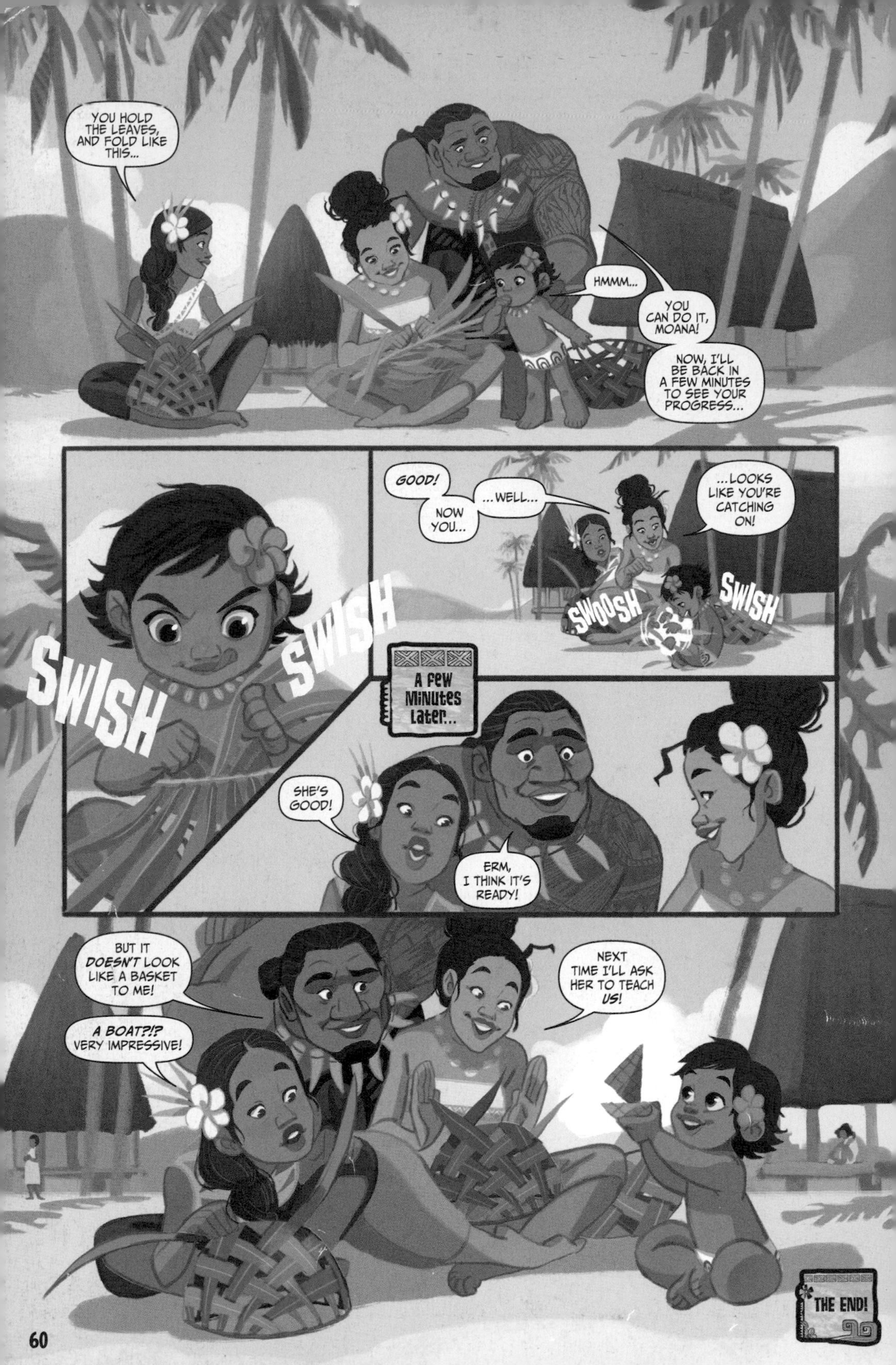
YOU HOLD THE LEAVES, AND FOLD LIKE THIS...
HMMM...
YOU CAN DO IT, MOANA!
NOW, I'LL BE BACK IN A FEW MINUTES TO SEE YOUR PROGRESS...
SWISH
SWISH
GOOD!
NOW YOU...
...WELL...
...LOOKS LIKE YOU'RE CATCHING ON!
SWOOSH
SWISH
A FEW MINUTES LATER...
SHE'S GOOD!
ERM, I THINK IT'S READY!
BUT IT *DOESN'T* LOOK LIKE A BASKET TO ME!
A BOAT?!? VERY IMPRESSIVE!
NEXT TIME I'LL ASK HER TO TEACH *US*!
THE END!

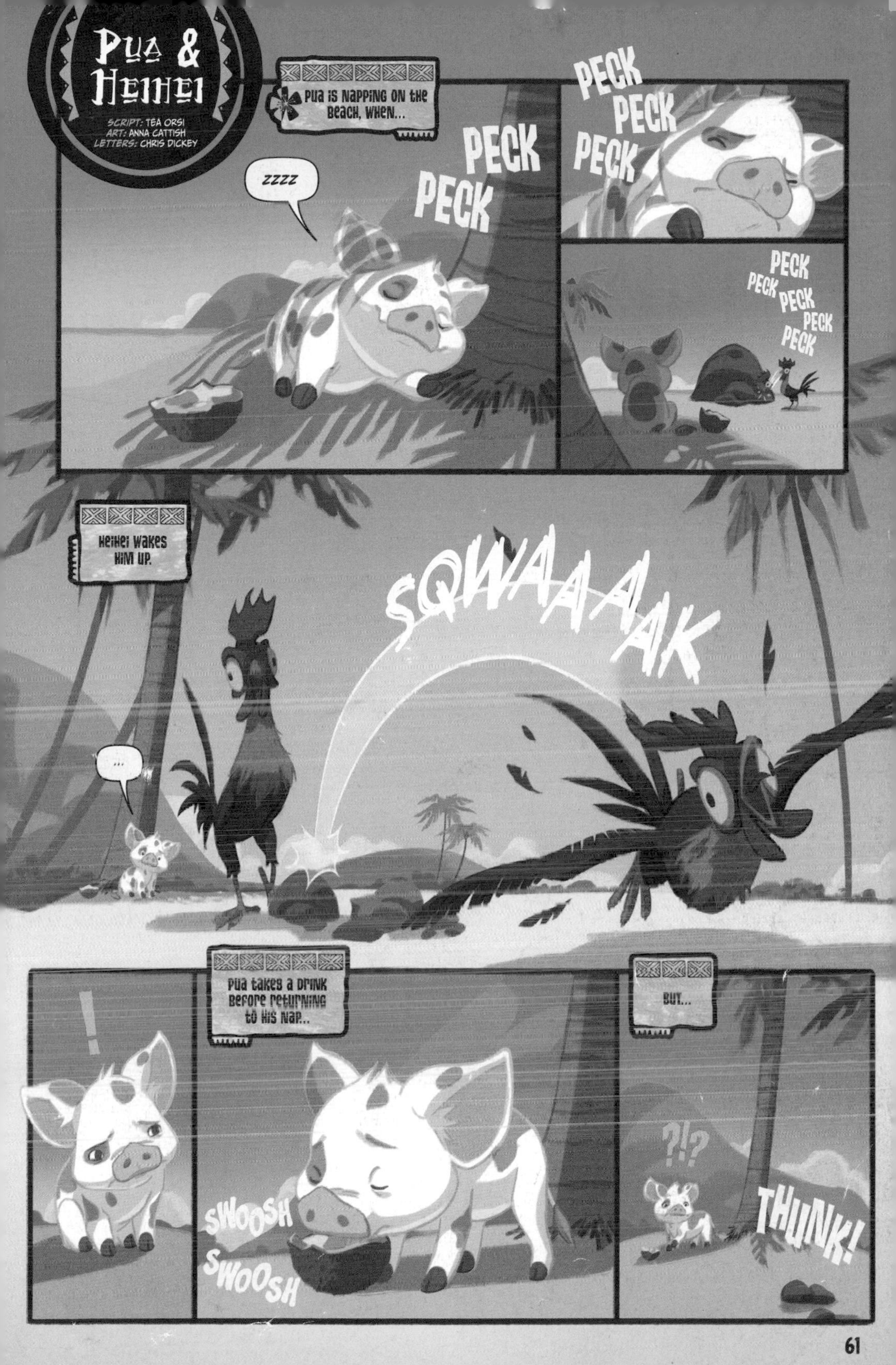
PUA & HEIHEI
SCRIPT: TEA ORSI
ART: ANNA CATTISH
LETTERS: CHRIS DICKEY
PUA IS NAPPING ON THE BEACH, WHEN...
ZZZZ
PECK
PECK
PECK
PECK
PECK
PECK
PECK PECK
PECK
PECK
HEIHEI WAKES HIM UP.
...
SQWAAAAAK
!
PUA TAKES A DRINK BEFORE RETURNING TO HIS NAP...
SWOOSH
SWOOSH
BUT...
?!?
THUNK!

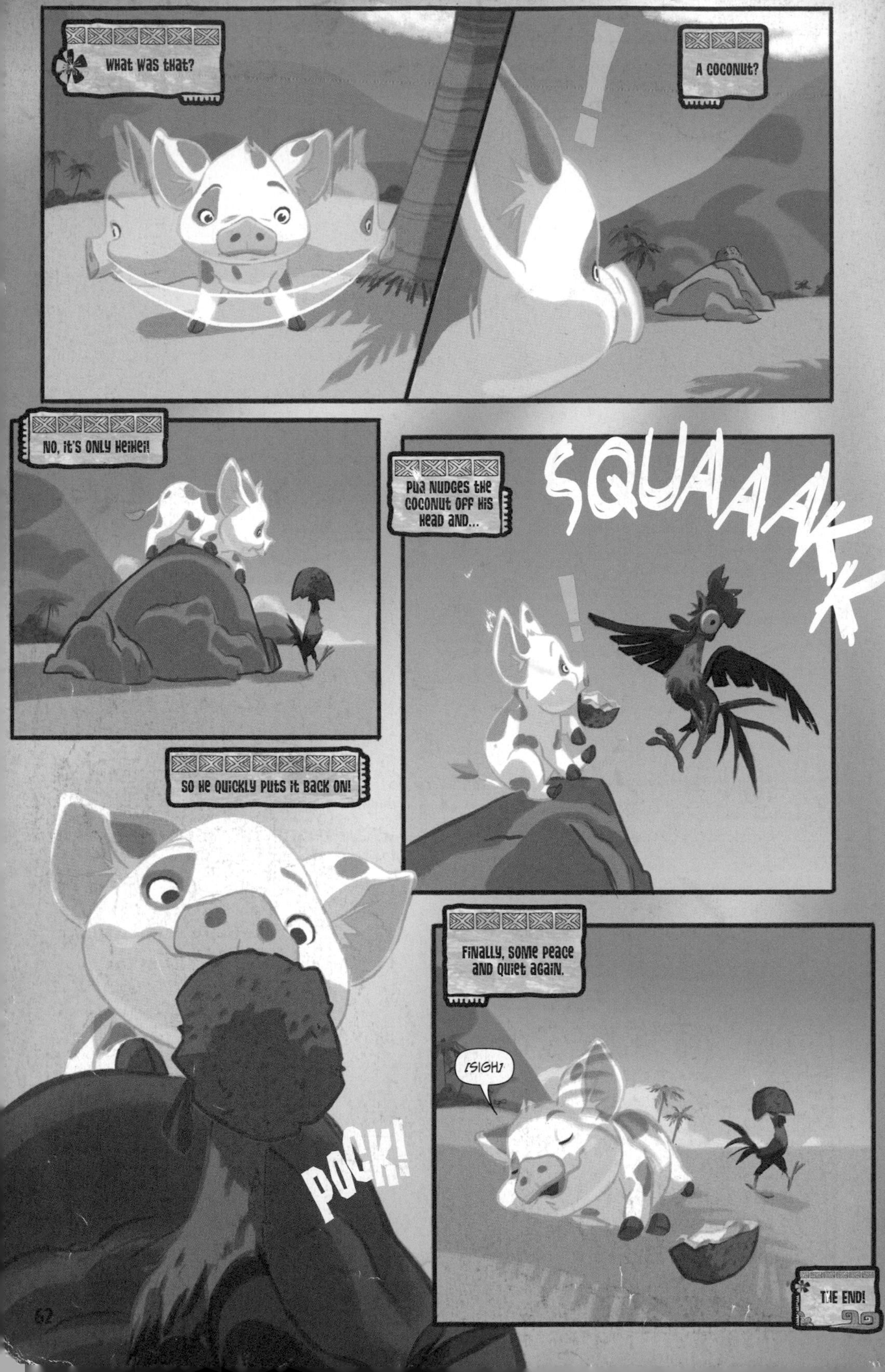
What was that?
A coconut?
No, it's only Heihei!
Pua nudges the coconut off his head and...
SQUAAAKK
So he quickly puts it back on!
POCK!
Finally, some peace and quiet again.
[SIGH]
THE END!

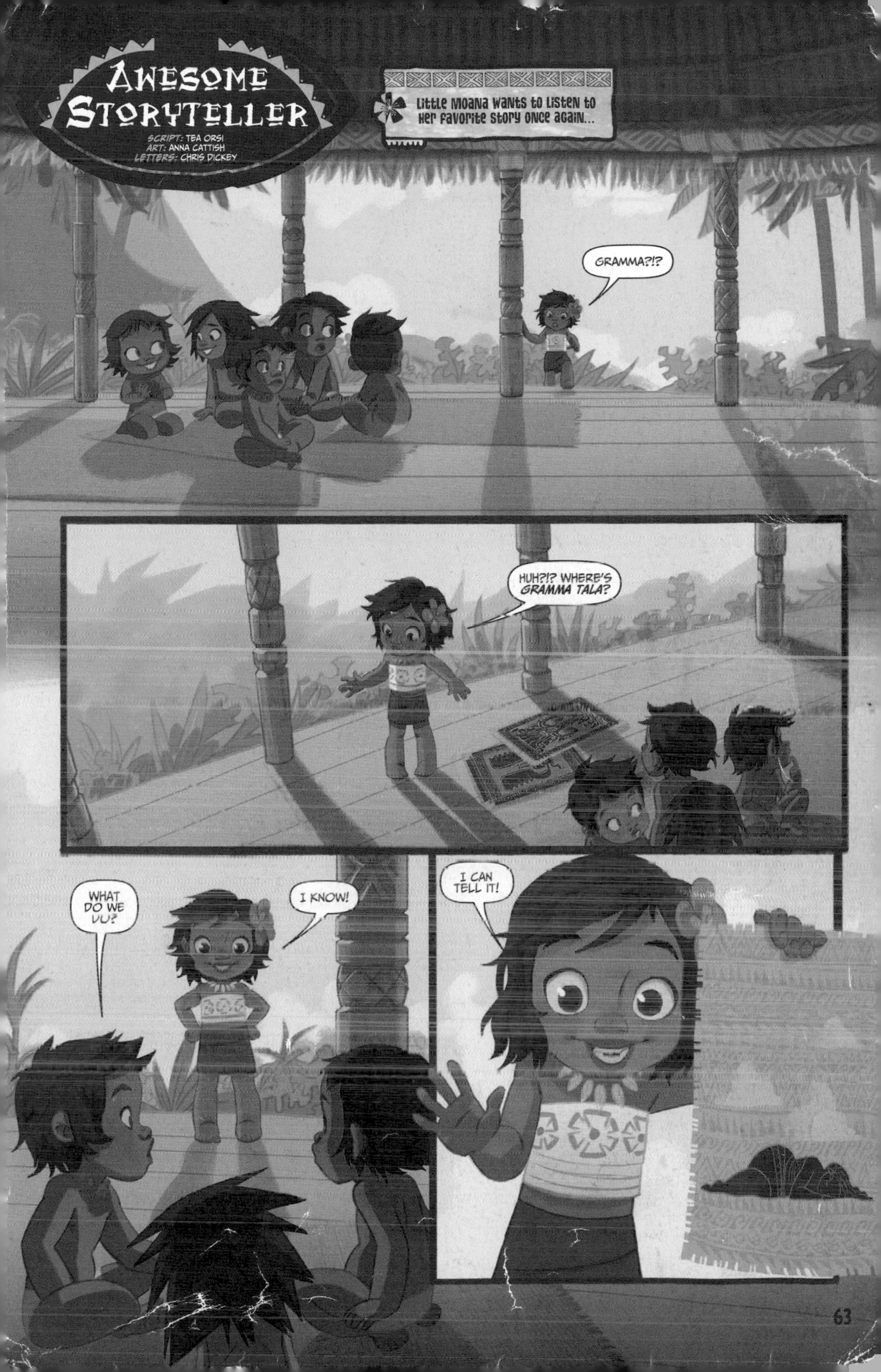
AWESOME STORYTELLER
SCRIPT: TEA ORSI
ART: ANNA CATTISH
LETTERS: CHRIS DICKEY
Little Moana wants to listen to her favorite story once again...
GRAMMA?!?
HUH?!? WHERE'S GRAMMA TALA?
WHAT DO WE DO?
I KNOW!
I CAN TELL IT!

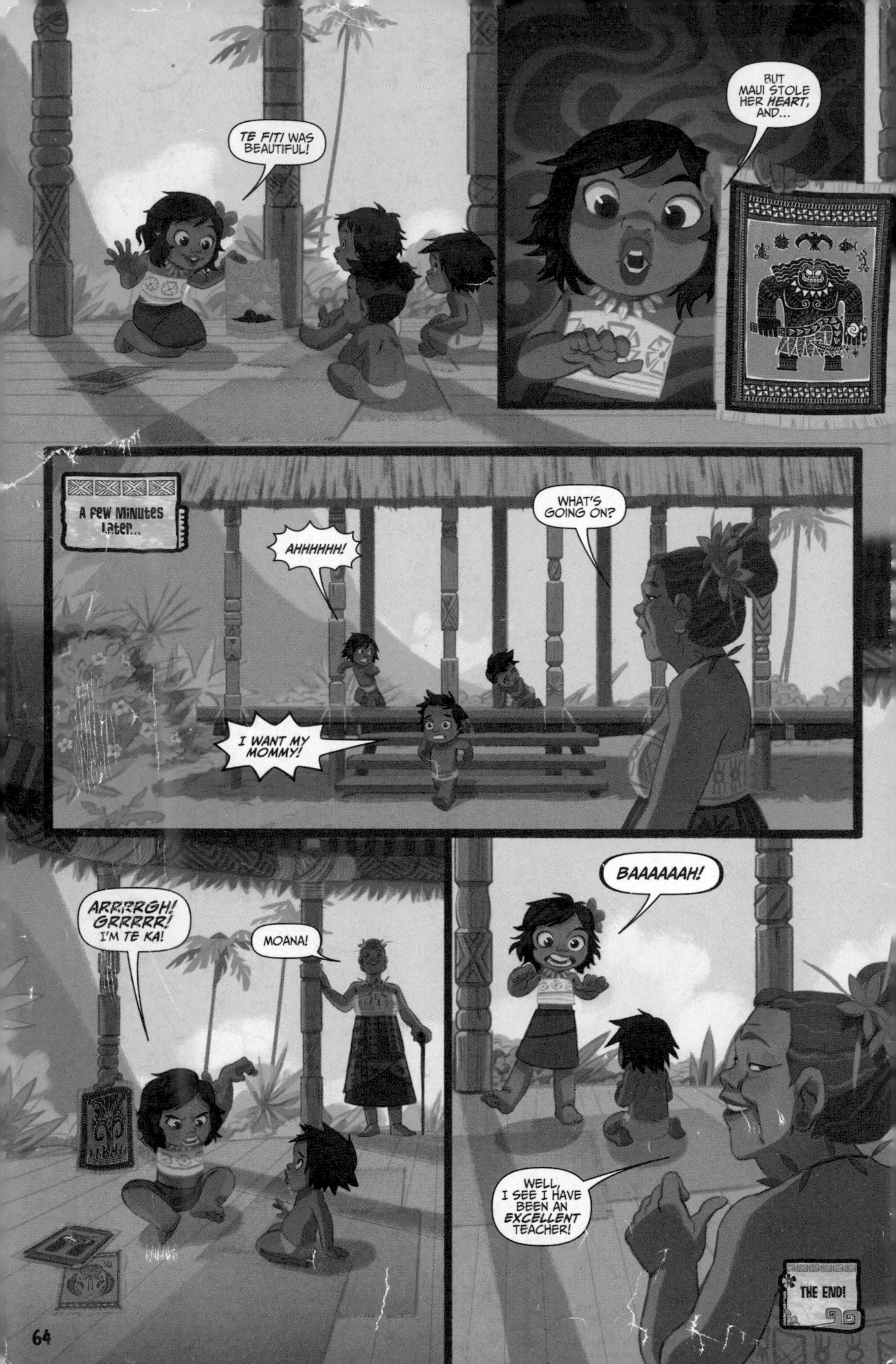

TE FITI WAS BEAUTIFUL!
BUT MAUI STOLE HER HEART, AND...
A FEW MINUTES LATER...
AHHHHHHH!
WHAT'S GOING ON?
I WANT MY MOMMY!
ARRRRGH! GRRRRR! I'M TE KA!
MOANA!
BAAAAAAH!
WELL, I SEE I HAVE BEEN AN EXCELLENT TEACHER!
THE END!